Mᴀʀᴛɪɴ Eɢʙʟᴇᴡᴏɢʙᴇ

THE WAITING

lubin & kleyner
london

The Waiting

first published in 2020 by lubin & kleyner

Copyright © Martin Egblewogbe, 2019
Cover Image © Eric Gyamfi, 2014
Author Photo © Kajsa Hallberg Adu, 2019
Cover Design © D237, 2019 | www.d237.com

This book is typeset in Union and Palatino from Linotype GmbH

lubin & kleyner, london
an imprint of flipped eye publishing
www.flippedeye.net

ISBN: 978-0-9541570-7-4

Praise for *The Waiting*

"Martin Egblewogbe's new collection, *The Waiting*, establishes him as the intellectual's short story laureate. These tales are book club set pieces - Indeed some titles alone are good for discussion sessions of their own. The humour of his earlier work is still present, but it takes a back seat to the riot of ideas that animate these tales. The human experience is shed on Egblewogbe's signature tales in redolent shavings of life. Innocuous words and sentences add up to chilling paragraphs which build up into haunting stories sited at the junction of normalcy, absurdia and fantasia. These characters, driven by their demons are forever searching - whether for love or for meaning - and forever failing to find; but their forlorn, comic and sometimes Kharmic journeys resonate in our experience."

Chuma Nwokolo, author of *The Exctinction of Menai*

"In this breathtaking collection of short stories, Martin Egblewogbe continues to demonstrate the brilliance he announced with his first collection, *Mr Happy and the Hammer of God & Other Stories.* Egblewogbe has created in *The Waiting* a rare work of art that is hard to categorize, not simply for its fecund descriptions, but more so because of a stylistic originality that transcends pigeonholing. Egblewogbe's subject matters range from the simple, though far from simplistic, to the almost metaphysical. He is as adept in covering the shenanigans of a pastor in *The Going Down of Pastor Muntumi*, with Maupassantian irony, as he is with the existential scope of a story such as *The Cwroling Caterpillar*, managing to achieve the tricky balance of imbuing his stories with sufficient cultural allusions to ground them, without rigidly tethering them to time and place."

Benjamin Kwakye, author of *The Sun by Night*

THE WAITING

MARTIN EGBLEWOGBE

Contents

A Photograph Of K & S, Smiling 9

Mekrema Fails The Flash Fusion Test 21

The Going Down of Pastor Mintumi 27

The Gonjon Pin 51

The Making 69

Rain 79

Back To The Halls 83

Atta 89

The Waiting 105

The Penitent 127

The Cwroling Caterpillar 135

A PHOTOGRAPH OF
K & S, SMILING

Hᴇ ᴅɪᴅ ɴᴏᴛ go into the outhouse just because he wanted to snap out of a growing idleness and propensity to remain in bed. On the contrary, it was something he had long planned to do, and it was his intention to return to bed as soon as it was done. He had planned to do it all those years while cursing the bitter Chicago cold and dreaming about a return to Ghana, to establish himself at home, to live the rest of his life in comfort, peace and quiet. K's original plan, though suffering fluxions and adjustments, followed a fairly predictable trajectory as the young African strove in the USA, not quite failing, not quite rising, but getting by – with prospects.

In the end things took an unexpected turn. Death, the master of the unexpected, struck. Though, in moments of reflection, it did seem to K that there was no death that could not be expected, no demise that could not be anticipated, not after thousands of years of the recorded human experience. The trope of the unexpected death was therefore, K concluded, only a feature of the shock of it all, the fact of the passing, the eternal removal, of his father in this case, his mother having been long since gathered to God. His American fortune was only half made, but his father had left him the old house, and so he could not close shop hurriedly enough, could not bid Chicago goodbye fast enough, the jet could not race through the clouds quickly enough, the engines could not burn hot enough, nothing was working hard enough but soon enough the rubber was hitting the tarmac at Kotoka – a bad landing, a bounce, a slight roll, and the 737 rolled to rest, and indeed there was K disembarking. The hot blast of dry air swept across his face. And, after seven and one half years, here was Ghana again.

The old man had already been buried. No need to hurry back, his uncle said to K over the telephone. He's really dead and you can't have a conversation no matter how hard you try.

K paid his first last respects to an old photograph of the man, taken in his prime, a portrait featuring a severe look and a thin moustache. That was not how he remembered his father. K Senior had been warm, even if of a rather reticent disposition, and incredibly considerate, as a sign of which he had asked to be buried in the garden. That was where K paid his final last respects, head bowed for ten minutes in silence before the tombstone. Then he made the sign of the cross and went into the house.

Not much had changed there since his childhood. The low-seating sprung armchairs that his father had designed himself, and which all agreed were very comfortable, were still there, the polish a little worn off on the arms, the dark red leather cracked in some places. The old Sanyo 21-inch black-and-white TV was still working by the power of God – what other power could have kept the device extant, built in

Ghana in 1975 and seeing with its grey phosphor screen an entire family rise and decay? What other power could make it so – that, after so many decades, pressing the switch still made the screen start to glow; by turning the dial a picture wobbled into life, and became sharp and clear, a woman reading the news, at 7.23 PM. K stood transfixed at the sight. Not even America, all new flat-screen TVs and bright colours and strangeness, could have prepared him for this. But on further reflection, reflected as he stood before the wooden box now glowing and resonating with sound, how could America prepare him for such a touching moment? For his experience over there had been one of shallowness.

Twenty years ago his father would be reclining in the chair, a glass of water beside him, the Bible in his hand. The TV would be on low volume, and K and his sister, Mansa, would be looking at the flickering screen.

Mansa had come to Ghana in time for the short illness, the death and the funeral. Even though a Canadian now, she had been *there when it mattered,* she told him on the phone – coldly accusatory, never mind that her presence in Ghana had been co-incidental with their father's demise. And were one to push it, K had thought as Mansa floated in her bullshit balloon over his head; who knows if your very presence precipitated the end? Of course there was a bit of jealousy in her attitude towards her, as she had done much better in life than he had. She had a string of degrees and a husband and a *career*, and he, at the end of the day, was just a hustler, another Ghanaian would-be emigrant and returnee. But he had saved some money and Daddy had left him quite a bit. He could at least rest for a while. Reflecting, perhaps.

But in those days in the distant past (but was it distant really?) they would play on the cold terrazzo floor – jig-saw puzzles and snakes and ladders – and perhaps ask Daddy to help with homework, until at 9.30 PM Daddy would rise, turn the TV set off, and send them to bed. When it was turned off, the Sanyo died with a loud crack! and a hiss as the screen glow collapsed to a white spot in the centre of the screen, which then faded, slowly, to black.

*

The great advantage of being possessed of a lack of ambition is the extended capacity to tolerate indolence without feelings of regret. Time, passing, is not seen as being lost, but rather being spent prudently, though one remained ensconced in an armchair, or reclining in a deck chair, or laid back in bed. It did not matter if the indolence were a natural tendency or induced, whether it be temporary or for life, the subject would invariably be capable of extended periods dedicated to doing nothing useful, a charge which K would decry: his indolence was not slothfulness, but an aid to philosophical reflection. In any case, a period of rest was something he deserved, K thought, after the unending hustle to make a life in America.

Winding up the affairs of the deceased, K had discovered that his father had bequeathed a fair amount of money, which, when added to K's savings, was enough capital to start some sort of business. The period of rest and reflection would be used to determine ways in which to invest this capital. It ran into weeks, this period of rest, which K spent in the house, reading, listening to music on the old Sanyo LP player, and reflecting. And K found that the allure of a life spent in philosophical reflection was great indeed.

*

There was a small single room outhouse behind the main building that served as a store-room. It was initially supposed to be a kind of servant's quarters, but the absurdity of that became clear to K Senior just before the construction started, and so he turned it into a tool-shed. It was absurd, he explained to his children, because

(a) they did not and would not keep servants

(b) that was a throwback from colonial times when the well-to-do had 'boy's quarters'.

So it became a shed for gardening tools and carpentry tools and tools for the car and so on. The rakes and cutlasses were placed in a cupboard in the near corner, to the right of the entrance, and the rest of the tools were arranged neatly on overhead shelves. This left a lot of space in the room, and slowly, it became a storeroom as well. Old toys that the children felt too attached to to throw away ended up there. There were cardboard boxes filled with old newspapers, magazines, and books. After the children completed secondary school, their suitcases, metal trunks, and chop-boxes ended up in this room as well.

There was a lot of history locked up in there.

So it was that one Thursday afternoon, after spending the entire morning in bed listening to Tchaikovsky, K decided to explore the store-room. He did it, not because he wanted to snap out of a growing idleness and apparent propensity to remain in bed. On the contrary, it was something he had long planned to do, and it was his intention to return to bed as soon as it was done. He was sure that it would help him in a major way to connect with the past and gain deeper insight into the events that had obviously defined his life, thus illuminating his future.

The keys were in the top drawer of the bureau in the living room, as they had always been. The key to the storeroom turned smoothly in the lock, as it always had, because K Senior had regularly greased all locks, because K Senior had always believed in keeping things in good shape. For the same reason the door, of course, swung open without creaking, but, bucking the trend, the lamp dangling on a crooked wire from the ceiling did not light up when K threw the switch. He left the door open and opened the little window at the opposite end. It was high in the wall, about a foot-and-a-half across. A shaft of bright light cut through swirling motes of dust and struck the floor, making a bright little square on the harsh grey concrete. There were boxes and bags and all sorts of nkukunkaka present, all decaying slowly in the long silence: parts of an old wooden bed taken apart and stored in a neat pile, a stack of chairs, a chest of drawers. A wry smile played on K's lips as he looked around – and his eyes lit on a metal trunk, all black with a motif of little red crescent moons stencilled across it. His name was spelt in little white letters across the front. A short sharp pain shot through his chest, making him jerk upright. That was his trunk! For three years of his life in the boarding house, it had contained all his most precious belongings. And after secondary school it had been stored here, and he had kept in it... things.

A bitter taste rose into his mouth as he walked across to the trunk and dragged it into the little square of light. He squatted beside the metal box and jerked at the lid. It opened with a loud shriek. A musty smell rose to meet his nose. It was a sickly-sweet smell that made him want to puke, but he shut his eyes and clenched his teeth, and in another moment the wave of nausea was over. His notebooks were arranged in a neat pile in one corner, and there were a number of yellowing orange folders that he recalled contained all his term reports, bills, and school correspondence. He reached for the first notebook. The word 'English' was neatly written in blue ink after 'SUBJECT:', which was printed in bold black letters. Below that was his name. He put it aside and reached for the next, which was his mathematics notebook. When he opened it, a silverfish scurried off the page and fell back into the trunk. The header on the page was 'Quadratic Equations', and there were many lines of text below. K dropped the book. Memories were flooding into his head. Oh those days! The miseries, the joys, the foolery, the potential, the waste, the... He sat on the floor, in the dust. He put his head in his hands. There was too much to remember, and most of it he would rather not. And yet, when else? If he was to face his past, why not start now? Because, he whispered to himself, those were the worst years of my life, the fucking years that were the foundation of the sadness that followed... If only he had known then what he knew now. And yet. He reached for an unmarked envelope tucked away beside the wall of the trunk. It was not sealed, and he slid the contents out. A bunch of photographs.

And there was a photograph of K and S, smiling. The shot had been taken outside this very house, just beside the gate and under the almond tree. They were looking up into the lens, bright-eyed, cheerful, posing with hands across each other's shoulders. Where was S now? He had moved out of the city just after secondary school, and K had not heard from him since. Yet, what was technology there for? K dug his iPhone from his trouser pocket and fired up his Facebook. His 845 friends, most of whom he had never met in person, would be milling about online wasting their time, but there were a few that might help him connect with S. But first a search, which yielded a profile of S, unmistakably S in the photograph, all chubby faced, a baby in his arms, and his profile said, Current city: Sunyani. Married to: Diana O—. Having absorbed this update of S's current circumstance, and having decided against contacting S directly via Facebook (why, the man could simply *ignore* his post, and what could he do then, but fret?), K sent a message to an acquaintance of theirs who was online at that very moment.

> *By any chance do you have a phone number for S? I need to get in touch pronto. (1:52 PM)*

Even though the little green dot on the screen indicated that this man was online, it still took him several minutes to reply to K's query. This did not bother K. He went on poking about in the trunk until a beep made him reach for the phone again.

> *Lol, what do you want him for? (2:09 PM)*
>
> *Whaddya think (2:10 PM)*
>
> *Here you go: 054 4 *** *** (2:15 PM)*

And that was it. K sat still for another ten or so minutes, trying to calm his nerves with a combination of heavy breathing, nuking his thoughts, counting down and counting up, and trying not to remember. But it did not work. That singular event was drawn up again, as it had been a million times over, and it replayed itself all over again.

S had turned up at K's house on a Saturday morning. It was in early January, schools were not yet in session, and dust from the harmattan hung still in the air. Oh, the memories of that early teen age! They conversed about school, their expectations for the coming term. And how they had spent the Christmas past, and it went well, the conversation, full of the innocence and honesty of childhood friendship. S had to leave after an hour, a book was to be collected from another friend, an older boy in Secondary School. It had not been K's intention to go with S on this visit to Y's house. However, that is what happened. K went to see S off, as was customary. And it so happened that the two friends were taken up in conversation as they trod the dusty path out of K's neighbourhood and crossed the road into S's plushier neighbourhood.

K laid the photograph on the floor and stood up, so that the beam of light from the window fell across his chest, and his head was in the shadow. He had not been dressed to go out that morning. In any case, their family was not rich at that time and Mansa and K's clothes were usually threadbare and marked with patches. His feet were clad in a worn pair of chale wote and his shorts must have sagged because he was not wearing a belt. His favourite home T-shirt, light-blue in colour, had an enlarged neckline from age and constant washing, and was threadbare around the armpits so that part of his bony chest could be seen. S, on the other hand, was well dressed. His sneakers were new, his corduroy trousers well pressed, and he wore a short-sleeved red and blue chequered shirt, neatly tucked in. His hair was oiled and combed, he smelt clean and rich. In the warmth of friendship, though, this disparity was of no importance and their conversation carried well, with smart quips and laughter, until S was pressing the door bell, an Alsatian was giving a deep-throated bark, and the tall, black metal gate was creaking open. They were ushered inside by a gate-man who was dressed as well as S was.

The house was a mansion, with sprinklers throwing jets of water over lush lawns. There was a white Mercedes in the driveway. The serene garden seemed to temper the rays of the sun and make them mellow and a calming hush descended as if to preserve a delicate thing of art, and it all took K's breath away and suddenly, forcefully, made him aware of how shabby he looked.

The gate-man led the two boys to a large veranda in front of the house, half concealed behind a green barrier sprouting from a row of white flower pots.

"How good to see you!"

The voice heralded the appearance of a slim woman wearing a wine coloured robe with a pearl necklace around her neck. "You must want to see Y?" she asked. "Yes," S replied. A few words of greeting were exchanged between them. K, ignored completely, hung back a few steps behind S, a confused smile playing on his lips.

"Come," said the woman. "You can wait here for him." It seemed that she was speaking only to S, but suddenly she seemed to notice K. "Excuse me," she said.

K did not understand. In the few seconds that must have elapsed, what had really occurred in his mind? What cues had he picked? Because it seemed to K that he was being asked to 'excuse them', quite literally. And, since he was not one to impose himself, he quietly stepped back, and was soon outside the gate, which was opened for him.

Standing outside, he still did not understand. Had he been thrown out? Did the woman just want to speak discreetly to S? And in his confusion he loitered about the house in the hope that S would come and fetch him, or that S would conclude the visit and come out. But nothing happened, and perhaps an hour passed? Then K went home.

It was an incident that had haunted K ever since.

Over the years, even as their friendship waned, K could not bring himself to ask S what had happened that day. Had he had been thrown out, or what? S neither spoke about the incident nor made reference to it, and by the time their ways diverged and S moved to another city, this had become the stuff of nightmares for K.

In later years K analysed the situation thoroughly. Most likely the woman had thought him some impoverished rascal not worthy of her presence; a poor, dirty kid who had no business in her house, an uncultured tyke whose presence could only besmirch her beautiful, beautiful son. And so it stayed, this conclusion, a permanent hurt in the heart much like the broken tip of a dagger left lodged in the flesh, often forgotten, inflicting pain and distress afresh when the muscles were tensioned in some manner.

But now, perhaps, was the time to get it all settled. A simple question for S, a simple answer from S, would make all the difference. But would S remember it, seeing as the event might have had so much less significance for him? But why not, thought K. A little prodding, and memory would bring it all up. And what if S lied about what had happened, or what if S succumbed to false remembering? And what if, and what if. Yet one would never know, if one did not try. Taking a deep breath, he hit the number, and heard the ringing, beep-beep, beep-beep.

"Hello, S here."

And after so many years, how was one to reply? Culture dictated the opening greetings, the exchanges of niceties. Decorum dictated a limit to probing, imparted a congratulatory disposition to the conversation. And yet, soon enough, all that began to fray and the question below the surface to chafe: *why have you called me?*

K cut to the core of the matter.

"Do you remember, that afternoon many years ago, you came to my house and we went to visit Y?" he asked. His voice trembled a little when he began, but firmed up again by the last three words.

"Yes."

"Did you get to see him?"

"Yes."

"You remember what happened, when his mother came out to greet you?"

There was a pause. Then, S replied in the same tone as before,

"Yes."

"What happened next?"

"You mean you can't remember? You remember everything else, except that?"

"I have never been able to understand what happened next."

S did not say anything.

"I mean, it's bothered me ever since. Did the woman ask me to leave?"

S did not say anything.

"Did she ask me to leave her house, and if so, why? That is what I can't understand. It's bugged me ever since, damaged my sense of self-worth, my self-confidence. Messed me up in ways you cannot imagine. It would be very helpful for me to bring this matter to closure. I should have asked you this a long time ago, but..." as his voice trailed off, K heard S clear his throat.

"You know," said S, slowly, gravely. "You're just a piece of shit. Always were." And S hung up.

And so the matter remained unresolved.

MEKREMA FAILS THE FLASH FUSION TEST

Mekrema had left his tailored jacket in the car, but the white shirt hugging his muscular chest and the free-swinging dark blue necktie were enough to identify him to anyone as a man in the wrong place, at the wrong time. His black shoes had been shiny when he stepped out of the car, but had since become coated with a thick layer of dust. His trousers had taken on an extra shade of grey. Once in a while a car or a truck sped past him, headlamps momentarily lighting up the dark, the vehicle bumping and rattling through the ruts and potholes, raising clouds of dust that billowed and then fell slowly back to the ground. His white shirt had become streaked with the red dirt, and the grit chafed where the collar met his neck. Sweat wet his armpits even though the weather was not very warm. When he glanced up he saw, towards the south, a single star that had managed to shine through the harmattan haze, yet it was a poor companion, this star. A poor companion, thought Mekrema.

He was in one of those incomplete neighbourhoods on the outskirts of the metropolis where the roads wove between grand, well-lit mansions and abandoned projects with partly-raised walls overgrown with weeds, home perhaps to local layabouts, or to small animals.

There was no moon that night, but the darkness was lightened by the myriad lights that shone upwards from the great city, caught and scattered through the atmosphere by the enshrouding harmattan.

Mekrema had no idea where he was going. The road led on, as all roads do, and he followed, as all who follow roads must do. A cog must have skipped in his thinking and his mind was stuck in an impossible loop. This perhaps was a momentary lapse in cognitive capacity for the smart young lawyer on the up and up: one foot after the other and nothing more complicated than that, one foot after the other.

And yet earlier in the day Mekrema had been studying a dossier of dozens of briefs and financial statements for a troubled client, and only a few hours later... The tricks life can play! Mekrema and his star, the lone yellow survivor in the sky. Earlier, when he stepped off the main road, there had been more people around. At the junction where the dirt road met the tarred road, there was a cluster of shops and a taxi station. Three battered vehicles stood in line, yellow fenders made tan by the endless, endless dust. The drivers were sitting on a bench having an argument, broken up by the arrival of prospective passengers: a woman with a baby strapped to her back and a small boy alongside. Not far from the junction, loud music blasted from a shop selling electrical appliances. Some of the other shops had radio and television sets on. There were many people about, happy, care-free. The noise distressed him. He thought about the peace and quiet of his home at Ringway Estates, and his office in Ridge.

Mekrema loitered for a while at the junction, shifting his weight from one foot to the other, shifting towards the cardinal points in turn, then walking slowly to the row of shops, where he met a man in a red shirt made of a material that shimmered in the fluorescent light. The man said something to the shopkeeper and the shopkeeper laughed. What was it that he said? Merry Christmas perhaps, Peace to the World and Goodwill to Man. Mekrema turned from the tarred road onto the dirt track and walked. Soon he had put a hundred meters between himself and the junction and the noise was fading away, and then he had put two hundred meters between himself and the junction and the road was quite deserted, and he walked on. At either side of the road the shrubs shook in the wind, making a friendly rustling, and the dark shapes tossed this way and that. There was a scattering of trees standing sentinel, rising here and there, way into the distance.

Mekrema was not quite sure what it was that attracted him to the place so far down the road, where the noise had died and the houses were few. From the road side the place looked like a wooden kiosk. The space in front of it was enclosed within a shoulder-high fence made of slats of wood painted in stripes of blue and white. A thatched roof slanted down almost to a man's height at the entrance to the enclosure. It was an awning, technically, but he had never seen an awning made of thatch, so perhaps it was better called a roof. As he drew closer Mekrema saw that the place was some sort of drinking bar, and he drifted towards the entrance and pushed past the curtain of bamboo beads that served as a door.

What had attracted Mekrema to the place? Perhaps it was the small yellow lamp outside, dimming and brightening for no apparent reason and with no clear rhythm. He had seen it from a distance, and as he approached he knew deep within, that this was the final destination, this was the place where he had to be, on the night they lied that Christ was born. Perhaps it was a rebirth, for, as he pushed through the bead curtain at the entrance, he knew at last that this was the place, the place. It was the place where men came to be punished.

The first thing that Mekrema noticed as he pushed the curtain aside was that the place smelled. It smelled of akpeteshie, it smelled of cigarette smoke, it smelled of marijuana smoke, and it smelled faintly of piss. The next thing that Mekrema noticed was that the place was badly lit, the only illumination coming from an incandescent lamp dangling over the counter immediately opposite the entrance. The third thing that Mekrema noticed was that the place was quiet. It had been quiet outside too and so he did not notice this immediately, but the place was a bar – a drinking spot! and Mekrema was surprised to find a drinking spot brooding in silence, contrary to popular knowledge.

An old man wearing a battered green fedora sat at the counter, playing a game of oware with himself. The otherwise grim silence was broken only by the gentle clacking as the marbles hit the bottom of a hemisphere. Mekrema stood at the counter, uncertain. The ceiling lamp was smudged with grime, so that it shone brighter in some spots than others. The bartender looked at Mekrema. He did not smile nor speak, his face remained blank. The shelves behind the counter carried few bottles – five or six only, Mekrema saw, and they were all unlabelled. A flailing thought ran through Mekrema's mind. A cider, he almost asked, but of course there was no cider in this place, there could be no cider in this place. The hopelessness of the situation must have showed on his face. The bartender held up three fingers: Fore, Middle, Ring. A cloud of misunderstanding quickly passed over Mekrema's face and he nodded. The man poured three measures of a drink – dark, cloudy – and handed the squat glass to Mekrema. The thing smelled like something meant to be poured into the engine of a tractor. There was a pause, and man faced man in the place where men came at last to be punished, and Mekrema again knew, as it were subliminally, that there was only one way in which the ritual was performed, and he drank steadily to finish in one gulp, and fire came from his nostrils and tears stung his eyes and he knew that it was all over, here he was at last in the place where all troubles were consolidated and made as one.

Mekrema turned to find a seat, and his eyes, now adjusted, saw a haphazard scattering of chairs, and figures like shadows in the grainy light. They were not playing in this place. Everybody was dead serious: the man slumped by the door in a stupor, the youth standing by the wall with a cigarette in his hand, now and then mumbling, mumbling, what was he mumbling, Mekrema could not make out the words but he knew that he would know what the man was saying even if he was speaking in a language Mekrema did not understand, for this was the place, where men came at last to be punished, no matter the sin this fact was clear, they were comrades in pain. Even the two men sitting face to face over the squat table, each examining, no, investigating, the features of the other's face and no one saying a word, they too were not playing, though it seemed that they were engaged in a competition to stare each other down. Soon enough Mekrema came to understand that they perhaps did not even see each other, buried as they were in the thing that brought them here, to this place that had taken them in a loving embrace, which the world had not offered, could not offer, would not offer, but there was always a place for people to go to: Joseph and Mary found the manger when the inn said no, and Mekrema had found the blue kiosk when the voice on the phone said I have been busy, and they did not speak of love, no, it had gone past that, no, the voice meant, no, and they did not speak of reasons, it was no, a last no, yet the voice did not say no, it lied and said work has kept me away.

Initially Mekrema wondered how he was going to pay for the drink. He had left his wallet in the car, along with his telephone. Would the old man wait for him to go and get his wallet? His tie, though dust-coated, was expensive enough to stand up drinks for everyone in the place – but would the bartender accept such payment? Obviously not. How about his wrist watch? Mekrema played with these thoughts until he understood that it was a foolish and unnecessary consideration, for the point of this place was not that he had to pay for the drinks, the point of this place was punishment, and that was the truth. A man need not pay for his punishment. Or did he? This was a ghastly proposition.

His car, now abandoned beside the road at a place that seemed a universe away, was last year's BMW 3 Series. A sleek machine, it had generated admiration among his peers and his status had climbed, his heart swelled with pride any time he saw it, not to mention when he stepped into it, or out of it, and heard the door shut with that world-famous *thn*. Driving it was sweet, it was a happy activity, the air-conditioning kept the car in a thrilling chill, and on the superb stereo, the sound was so smooth, so clear, so low, almost sub-aural, UB40 strummed and throbbed, and Mekrema had smiled as he pulled to the side of the road and placed the call. He had waited the whole day in anticipation – the whole week was it not? – indeed it had been a month, and it was all supposed to be nice and easy and full of joy and laughter, but this was not what happened. In one minute, or less, the world came to an end, and he sat there, the Nokia gleaming in his hand, and the message on the screen said DISCONNECTED, disconnected, but why was it disconnected? This was left for Mekrema to decipher.

At the counter, the bartender was expecting him again. This time he waited patiently for Mekrema to move, measuring glass gripped between thumb and forefinger, the bottle of absinthe in his right, and Mekrema's glass to his left. Mekrema held up five fingers. The correct attitude was not even one of sorrow, it was one of a deep and desperate indifference. The drink splashed into the glass.

THE GOING DOWN OF
PASTOR MINTUMI

CHAPTER 1, WHICH CONCERNS THE MANNER IN WHICH
MINTUMI SPENT A SATURDAY EVENING.

An ageing incandescent bulb cast an unholy blue hue over
the cheap furniture placed perfunctorily about the small
room. The armchair in the corner had a sagging bottom, and
the surface of the small table was pitted with cigarette burns.
A rusty fan dangling from the ceiling creaked noisily as it
stirred the warm air, doing little to reduce the stuffiness. The
blades of the fan cast dancing shadows on the bed, whereon
two Members of the General Public were engaged in coitus.
The prostitute was tweaking Pastor Mintumi's right nipple,
her fingers sliding smoothly through the thick hair on his
sweaty chest. Mintumi was not enjoying himself, although

he, avoiding the woman's face, stared at the ceiling with a glassy look easily mistaken for the herald of an imminent orgasm. Rather, Mintumi was wracked with thought as he clutched at the woman's flat bottom and humped away robustly. The prostitute was not enjoying herself either, this contributed to Mintumi's distress – for all his effort, he suspected that the woman was close to bursting out in derisive laughter, dismounting with a careless fart and making an ego-destroying statement like, 'your okro prick'. That night, Pastor Mintumi was convinced that he was an unfortunate man. He had long suspected that he was not exactly a lucky bloke, but as he lay on his back with the hag hovering over him, the fact became clear, as if it had been stencilled on the dirty, cobwebbed ceiling: MINTUMI YOU ARE AN UNFORTUNATE MAN.

To begin with, the woman was not even pretty. In his haste, he had ended up with a woman of indeterminate age with frighteningly large breasts and a small arse. These breasts now swung pendulously above him, as if warning him to be careful next time. Earlier on, he had foolishly said to the woman, in order to make the interaction seem more – social, perhaps – he said, as she removed her clothes, 'Your breasts look nice.' The woman, carelessly tossing into the wardrobe the bell-bottomed trousers which had helped conceal her spindly legs, had replied, 'But you know that I have two children.' Of course, Mintumi was supposed to know that she had two children, because, and this was the worst of the case, she was a member of his congregation.

Indeed, when the pimp had appeared beside his car with the woman, Mintumi's initial reaction was to pray for instant transfiguration – if even into a goat. He next considered making off at great speed, but this was out of the question because he was parked in a dark, narrow alley, and the car was facing a wall which would have brought him to grief had he attempted any fast moves. So Pastor Mintumi had been left with no option but to brazen it out. He racked up all his reserves of confidence, and even as his ears burned with shame, cleared his throat authoritatively and told the woman that he had extended his 'evangelisation' to one-on-one's with ladies of the night. Sadly, that did not wash with the hardened woman of the world. 'You pay money to preach, or to eat the thing?' the woman asked.

Mintumi blamed the pimp. He had paid the man to get 'nice girl for jigi-jigi' and the idiot had brought him an ugly hag from his own church. So, since the woman and himself were partners in sin, Mintumi decided to let go of pretence and admit that he was in fact there not to preach, but to eat the thing. The woman, whom everyone called Sister Betti on Sundays, tried to make him feel at ease by promising that she would 'never never tell anybody.' Sister Betti also invited him to become a regular customer, with the assurance of total secrecy and excellent service. The fact that Mintumi could not bear hearing these words, let alone consider their import, was lost to Sister Betti, who seemed elated to have landed such a catch – she, a fisher of men for the flesh, catching a fisher of men for the spirit. Negotiations with the pimp were rapidly concluded, and the couple zoomed off in his Touareg to the hotel, known for hosting such clandestine engagements. The receptionist, himself an old man who had seen too many sinners in his time, was apparently not only deaf, but dumb as well. But they did not need sophisticated sign language to tell him what they wanted.

Pastor Mintumi knew that all this was the work of Satan. It could not be otherwise. At home, his two children were certainly asleep. His wife too, would be asleep, no doubt comforted by the thought that her husband was engaged in some righteous enterprise for the Lord, while in fact the pattern over the past year was that at least once every month Mintumi would enter into the world of strange women.

And that was how come he found himself battling with the odour of sweat and perfume that pervaded the seedy little room, the blue light disguising the aged furniture, the naked Betti encompassing his vision. Intercourse came to a whimpering end, and Sister Betti released Mintumi from her clutches. Betti, sitting on the bed, watched him silently for a few seconds. Mintumi stole a glance at her, and he recalled the compact and powerful bodies of the young women he had contended with in the past, he recalled Mercy the chorister, and a bitterness wrung his bowels. Mintumi reached for his clothes and started dressing up. 'Why?' Betti asked. 'I've finished.' Mintumi said. Betti reached for her clothes reluctantly. As she strapped her mighty breasts into the bra, she suddenly turned to Mintumi struggling into his trousers at the other end of the room. 'I want more money,' she said. The pastor pushed his foot too hard into the trouser leg, lost his balance, and fell with an ignominious thud. Betti towered over him, blocking the glare from the lamp, so that Mintumi could not see her face. 'Haven't I tried for you?' she asked. Mintumi tried to speak, but all words eluded him, and he could only stare helplessly at the woman hovering over him. 'OK,' Betti said with an air of finality, and, to Mintumi's horror, unclasped her bra. 'Let's do it again,' she said. 'But you will pay more.' Mintumi leapt to his feet, drawing up his trousers in one move. 'No!' He screamed. His voice sounded unearthly, as if it crashed into the room from the ceiling. The woman looked frightened. 'Never!' Mintumi shouted again. He put on his sneakers without sitting down, keeping an eye on Betti all the time. 'It's over!' He declared, satisfied at the cowing effect of his words. 'Take your time,' Betti said softly, as Mintumi charged past her out of the door.

The night welcomed him with open arms, the chill breeze was a balm to his outraged senses. But when he got into his car he realised that his wallet was missing. He must have dropped it in the room. Mintumi's return to the reception was heralded by the swing doors crashing open: the pastor's eyes were red. The old man raised his head slowly to face the angry returnee. 'I want to go back to the room!' Mintumi said tersely, fighting the urge to shout out loud. The receptionist shook his head. 'I...' Mintumi started, his anger building to great levels. He would gladly have wrung the scrawny neck of the man, but then he remembered that the man was deaf and dumb – or at least was supposed to be deaf and dumb. Rudimentary sign language was of no use here. Mintumi ran down the corridor to the room he had just recently vacated with such relief. He tried the handle, but the door was locked. He kicked the panels and the noise crashed through the night, startling Mintumi himself. He stared at the door, sweat streaking his creased face. Words marched across the dirty panels AN UNFORTUNATE MAN MINTUMI TONIGHT YOU LOST MINTUMI AN UNFORTUNATE MAN... The pastor turned around. The old man was standing behind him, one trembling hand on a cane, the other raised as if to ward off a blow.

CHAPTER 2, WHICH CONCERNS THE MANNER IN WHICH BEGAN THE GOING DOWN OF MINTUMI.

There was a young man who, if appearances could be believed, was an exemplary member of the church. Dedicated to the growth of the church and committed to the cause of the gospel and what more could Mintumi ask? Masgo, for that was the man's name, always sat in the second row on the left of the aisle. He was always there. Whenever Mintumi stood behind the pulpit he could not escape Masgo's eyes, following his every gesture; when he looked away he could not escape Masgo's voice, reaching towards him with a 'Preach it, Pastor!' Yet, Mintumi always had niggling doubts about Masgo's sincerity, and could not get past the feeling that Masgo was making fun of him. Masgo was not too much of a handsome young man, but he did pay much attention to grooming. Twenty-nine or thereabouts Mintumi surmised. His skin was rather dark, his hair luxuriant but with a hint of baldness already, his nose, one of the things which made him not handsome, was too fat, bulbous, flat at the bridge, and his lips protuberant, but the lower more so than the upper. A sharp dresser, though. Starched white shirts, rose coloured silk ties, suspenders, designer suits. Not to mention his shoes, on which not a smudge of dust could be seen. The fact of the matter was that Mintumi was jealous, for reasons which will shortly become apparent.

Mintumi first noticed Masgo one Sunday, about two years ago. It was during testimony time, after he had delivered his sermon and prayed for the sick and so on. The testimonies began with the usual matters. A couple of old women confessed that they had been touched by his preaching, and their arthritis vanquished, they had danced kpanlogo during the 'praises and worship' session, yes, with no trouble at all and praise be to God, and a young woman spoke about receiving a marriage proposal after a week of fasting, a trader had received a visa to Italy, wasn't the Lord good, wasn't He, eh? But then Masgo came and did something quite different. He was a good speaker, and exuded confidence and charisma. Masgo spoke about the amazing effects of 'Jerusalem Holy Oil', which pleased Mintumi to no small end. This powerful, wonder-working oil was in fact was olive oil which the pastoral council had bottled and put on sale at the church as an 'anointing oil'. The entire consignment of one thousand bottles had been prayed upon by Mintumi, but the congregation was not patronising the oil as he would have wished. In a month, only sixty-eight bottles had been bought. Out of a church strength of more than five hundred! Mintumi was considering drastic measures. But then that Sunday Masgo took the microphone, praised the Lord, and proceeded to speak about the oil. It had brought him good fortune halleluyah, and helped him to escape from the snares of an enemy. And it appeared that Masgo, solely on account of the miraculous power of the 'Jerusalem Holy Oil', had become a staunch member of the congregation. The anointing oil sold out within the week. But, though initially Mintumi was glad to have Masgo in the church, he soon began to have that niggling feeling, that something was not quite right about this young man.

But the foregoing is only peripheral to the matter to be discussed in this section. One day a chorister, a member of the Chosen Generation Singers, as the church choir was called, came to see Mintumi in his office. Mintumi was engrossed in writing another book, *Eight Keys to the Kingdom*, a sequel to the well-received *Seven Steps to Secure Your Salvation*. Ever since he wrote his first book, *Only One Way to Heaven,* he had made sure to put out a title every year. When his second book, *Two Things You Need To Know About Tithing* was published, the response was very enthusiastic, and by the time he put out his third book, *Three Arguments For The Trinity*, he was sure that he had made a name for himself as an inspirational and Christian writer. He followed with *The Four Paths to Good Fortune, Five Ways to Recover Your Faith,* and *Six Techniques to Stay from Sexual Sin.* Mintumi had developed a routine for writing, and with strict discipline, worked on his books on Tuesday evenings, the one day on which his church did not have a service. The visit of a church member to his office, though not unusual, was unexpected, and initially, Mintumi was not pleased with the interruption. Mercy had some complaint or the other – the choirmaster had not selected her for a Gospel Music festival, or some such triviality. In any case, Mercy and the pastor ended up fondling each other, after which they proceeded to fornicate. Mercy shouted dirty words all the time that they romped about the office, unsettling the settee and scattering the cushions onto the carpet, bumping butts against the desk and knocking the picture of Jesus flat on its face. The encounter was hugely erotic beyond what mere lovemaking could generate, and in-between orgasms, Mintumi was so fired up that he could not rest, he held one end of his singlet and swung the garment around in grim silence while rocking his torso back and forth with a mad gleam in his eyes, while Mercy, ravished, lay breathing heavily on the carpet. It all came to an end at about nine that evening, and they left the church offices. Mintumi drove Mercy to her house, and they parted on excellent terms, though they both knew that such a thing could not happen again. It was so, that as Mintumi drove home that night, he felt strangely cheated by life. Such terrific fucking, he mused, was what some people had been enjoying since their teenage years. Not bothered by the spectre of hell and morality, and for some reason finding the right sort of partners, such terrific fucking, since their teenage years. And how many times a week! Or month! Or year! Take Masgo, for example. He, Mintumi knew, was one of those who led that kind of life. Oh, he could see through his pretensions! Were it not for the grace, lightning would sear Masgo's arse. Oh yes, Mintumi thought. And so Mintumi's jealousy of Masgo multiplied many times over, and a tinge of hatred crept into his heart, when he compared the life of Masgo to his own. And his wife, the calm and patient Millicent, fifteen years of marriage and still counting, and he never had had such sex, never! He recalled a recurring dream, in which a man in a pointed black hat appeared and yelled, '"This is the title of the book: *How Jesus Stopped Me From Marrying The Woman Of My Dreams*."' How could life be so unfair? Eh? Millicent, who approached the bed singing Wesleyan hymns, yet who could blame her, she was osofo yere but at last Mintumi knew the difference between hot sex and the rest, and thus began the going down of Mintumi.

CHAPTER 3, WHICH CONCERNS WHAT HAPPENED TO MINTUMI AFTER HIS WALLET WAS STOLEN AND HE STOOD AT THE DOOR OF ROOM 12, WITH THE DEAF AND DUMB RECEPTIONIST STANDING BEHIND HIM.

The soundscape of the corridor was settling down again after the perturbation of Mintumi kicking the door, and thumping it, once, twice, to no avail. The insistent buzz of the fluorescent lights re-asserted themselves, and the mysterious clickings and sighs of a building at night were audible again. But Mintumi could swear that he could hear people giggling in the rooms, wondering at the brouhaha but suspecting something amusing. The receptionist raised a gnarled hand... and Mintumi shrank, but the hand rose to the man's protuberant Adam's apple and gave it a gentle tweak, as if to fit it properly in place. And then Sister Betti turned the corner of the corridor, and approached Mintumi, and there was a man with her.

'Pastor!' she said, in a voice that was too loud. 'It is good that you are still here. Come, let's go.' A slow smile spread across the receptionist's face. Mintumi, though partly relieved at seeing Betti, wanted to know above all whether she had his wallet or not. But the whole thing was getting out of control. The man with Betti, a short man with a pot belly that wanted to destroy his belt, seemed to hide a smirk behind a bushy moustache. Mintumi could not now bring himself to ask, 'Where is my wallet?' for fear of further embarrassment, because of course Betti might shout for all to hear, 'Oh don't worry it is in my drosse,' or such, and that would not do at all. He followed Betti and the man back down the corridor, through the swing doors, and into the night. A rather stiff cool breeze had picked up, and Betti adjusted the shawl across her shoulders. They crossed the parking lot, passed out of the gates, and stood beside the road.

'Well,' Mintumi began. 'But you koraa why? Running away like that.' Betti interjected. 'As if you don't know me. As if I was kakamotobi. If I wanted to do something to you, wouldn't I have done it to you in the room? When I was on you? Eh?' The other man cleared his throat. 'It is phlegms,' he said apologetically. 'Actually, I can't find my wallet,' Mintumi said. 'It is with me, come and let's go.' Betti said. 'Why don't you just give it to me now? I have to go home.' The man cleared his throat again. 'It is phlegm,' he said. He coughed. 'I went to put it in my room,' Betti said. 'For safe keeping. It is not far. Let's go.' And she led the march, three shadows cast by the street lighting along the main road, and then after a minute a left turn into a dark side street further along which the smell of decaying piss destroyed the olfactory tranquillity delivered by the freshness of the pre-dawn breeze. They were accompanied by the sad tramping of six feet on the gravel, and no one spoke, and then there was another turn, and another, and after five minutes Mintumi was lost, and after eight minutes he was hopelessly lost, and after ten minutes they passed through creaky metal gates into the courtyard of a compound house. The ubiquitous fluorescents burned away on the eaves of the building, which was long, like a classroom block, with several doors along the length. There was a wing to the left, and a wing to the right. The courtyard was paved, but with rough and uneven concrete slabs. A small group of women sat outside one of the rooms, and their conversation dropped when the trio entered. Betti led Mintumi and the other man across the yard and past a row of barrels for storing water, which were lined against the wall. Betti paid no attention to the other women. But Mintumi, whose ears were sharp, caught the whispers: 'Ei... abrewa power... This one for short, or for sleep?' and the hushed laughter as Betti threw open the door to one of the rooms and pushed Mintumi inside. 'Stay here, I'm coming,' she said brusquely, and he heard the door lock behind him.

The room was surprisingly large, and served both as a living room and a bed room. In the front of the room two armchairs and a settee sat around a large coffee table, and behind this arrangement a queen size bed receded into the shadows. There was a dresser to the side of the room, and beside it, a bureau with two chairs in front of it. Two men were seated in these chairs, facing each other. Even though they saw Mintumi's entry and his state of confusion, they continued to talk as if nothing had happened.

One of the men, tall and lanky, sat with his legs crossed, and an elbow on one knee. He was reading aloud from a sheet of paper in his hand. And then Mintumi recognised the other man, and his legs gave way, and he crumpled to the ground, and his cheek kissed the cold linoleum.

The other man was the church photographer.

CHAPTER 4, WHICH CONCERNS WHAT HAPPENED TO MINTUMI
IN BETTI'S HIDEOUT.

'This medicine will really be powerful ooo,' the photographer said, speaking in his lazy, unbothered tone. 'I bet you,' the tall man replied. 'Listen to this: "Because of the risk of serious hepatic toxicity, this medication should be used only when the potential benefits are considered to outweigh the potential risks, taking into consideration the availability of other effective therapy". You hear that? It is a medication of last resort. Now listen: "Posology and method of administration."' 'Poso – what?' the photographer asked. 'Posology,' the tall man said. 'Listen to the word even. What a medicine! Posology and method of administration. "Adults should take one tablet of 200 mg every day with a meal. Children, 15 to 30 kg should take one 100 mg tablet every day with a meal."' The photographer protested: 'But it said *Keep out of the reach of children*!' 'Just so!' the tall man agreed. 'How then can a child take the medicine, if it is kept out of his reach?' the photographer asked. 'You must think straight,' the tall man remonstrated. '"Out of reach", it said, not out of mouth. "Undesirable side effects,"' the man continued. '"Metabolism and Nutrition Disorders. Anorexia. Psychiatric and Nervous System Disorders..."' 'Yie,' the photographer interjected. 'It even affects the brain?' 'I told you it is not a small medicine,' the tall man said, looking at the medicine box in admiration. 'What a medicine,' he said again. The two men fell silent.

'The man is on the ground,' the photographer observed, after a while of this silence. 'Why, is he sleeping?' The tall man asked. 'I think he is waiting for Betti.' 'Why doesn't he sit down?' The other man did not reply. 'Why doesn't he lie on the bed, then?' 'Maybe has collapsed.' The tall man resumed reading aloud again.

Mintumi found no good reason to rise. The linoleum was dirty – he felt the grit on his cheeks and arms. He would be more comfortable seated in one of the chairs, but comfort was far from his mind. Presently he wondered whether the two men, engrossed in their analysis of medication advisories, would be able to help him find his wallet. Perhaps it was lying somewhere in the room, or even, Betti might have given it to them. There was danger, of course, in involving more people in the sordid details of this matter. At this time, to the best of his knowledge, all that the men knew was that Betti had thrown him into the room and left. That could be as a result of a wide range of possible events. Therefore, he could only try, perhaps, and he just might gain his freedom. The photographer presented a terrible difficulty. It was clear that the man had seen enough of him for definite identification, but had shown no signs of recognition. Why? But Mintumi could not answer this question, and decided to relegate it to the far background, and concentrate on getting his freedom. That matter could be tackled later.

'Gentlemen,' Mintumi called from his disadvantaged point on the ground, his lips just a centimetre shy of grazing the linoleum. 'Hei!' said the tall man. 'He is talking!' Mintumi was pained by this interruption. But before he could make another attempt at speech the door opened and Betti walked in. 'Why are you on the floor?' she asked, but her voice was flat and had no surprise in it. She sat in one of the armchairs. 'Get up. Here is your wallet,' she said, at the same time reaching into her bra and fishing out the leather pouch from underneath her right breast. She tossed the thing onto the table, where it landed with a soft thud and slid a few inches. As he raised himself up Mintumi was blinded by a brilliant flash, and as he turned towards the source the flash exploded again. The church photographer was on his feet, and he was lowering the brand new Canon Rebel SLR camera that the church had bought for his work. 'Asare! What are you doing?' Mintumi shouted at the photographer. 'What does it look like?' Betti sounded caustic. The tall man sauntered forward, with a dagger glinting casually in his hand. 'It is not hard to do a castration,' he declared. 'Just slit the scrotum, cut off the balls, tie the vas deferens. Over in two minutes. Depending on the length of the incision, sutures might not even be required.' The man sat down opposite Betti and grinned. His teeth were like fangs. Sweat dripped from Mintumi's face, but he felt cold, and was shivering. The tall man raised the dagger and tapped his teeth with the tip.

'Sweetie,' Betti said. 'Look how you are sweating. Is the room hot? Take off your shirt. Take off your trousers. You see the bed? Hehehe.' Betti unbuttoned her blouse and as her great breasts emerged Mintumi stepped backwards, trembling on rubbery legs. The room lit up with the camera flash. 'Take it off,' the tall man said. 'Take off your shirt, or I shall cut you. Take off your trousers, or I shall cut you. I will not say it again, but I will cut you if you make me stand up.'

Mintumi knew he was lost. He could not call for help, not even to God! Not even to Christ! Whom he preached! And button released followed button released, each arm was raised in turn and the shirt travelled to the ground, and the trouser zip slid downwards with no resistance, and each leg rose in turn and the trousers lay to the side. 'I will not hurt you,' Betti said. 'Business was good today. I am happy. I just want to talk. You see the bed? Hehehe.' The flash went off again. Mintumi wanted to scream to the photographer to stop it! 'Take off your boxer shorts,' the tall man said. 'Or I shall cut you.'

And so it happened, that Mintumi finally stood naked in the room and the photographer took pictures from all angles, circling the room. He paused to scroll through the pictures on the camera. 'The pictures are not bad,' he said. 'Let me see,' said the tall man, and the photographer bent towards the chair, and showed him the pictures. 'Yes, I see. Aha. They're OK. They're OK. Show them to Betti.' But Betti waved the photographer off. She looked carefully at the pastor, starting from his head and scanning his height slowly, to his feet. 'Pastor Pastor,' she said. 'Look at your okro prick.' And, as if under a spell, Mintumi lowered his eyes. His penis had shrunk to an unbelievable length, and his balls had almost vanished. Tears came into his eyes. Betti crossed her legs, the bell-bottomed trousers swished flamboyantly. 'Don't get us wrong, pastor. We all love you. We mean no harm. We just want to talk. Through your church, our lives have been improved. I will give your wallet back to you. But I will take the money out of it. Saman, take the money and count it. Asare, help Pastor to sit here beside me. He is looking too pale. Pastor, don't worry, eh? Saman, how much?' 'Four hundred cedis,' Saman declared, continuing with some disdain, 'Then some foolish papers. Then condom.' 'Eish, Pastor,' said Betti. 'So you have all this money and you only gave me forty cedis? Why? Is it a tithe? You were giving me tithe? Saman, take the money and put it down.' Mintumi was now seated beside Betti. He was no longer feeling cold, and the sweating had stopped. But he was still speechless. 'Oh Pastor, you are looking too fine. Let me hold you. Let me kiss you. Don't you like me? Eh? I am not fine?' She grabbed Mintumi, pushed herself against him, and kissed him. The camera went tic-tic-tic as the room was bathed in multiple flashes. 'Sweetie, I want to let you go home, to your wife, I am sure she is worried about you. Or don't you think so? You just give me your ATM number. Only that, and you can go.' Saman added, 'And if you don't give it to us, or if you give us the wrong number, I will cut off your balls. I am a veterinary assistant. This is what I do every day to animals.' While Mintumi considered this proposition, Betti stood up and put on her blouse, as if the issue did not concern her at all. 'Asare, bring Pastor his clothes,' she said.

Mintumi felt a strange, sour sense of gratitude when his clothes were handed to him, and he quickly dressed up, with Asare helping him when he missed a couple of buttons. But when he was done dressing up Betti asked him again for his ATM number. And Mintumi's tongue was loosed, and he sought to negotiate. 'Delete the pictures from the camera before I talk,' Mintumi said. 'Delete them?' the photographer replied. 'Why, I'll even give you the memory card.' The photographer extracted the little bit of plastic from the camera and tossed it onto the table. 'But if you give us the wrong number...' Saman began, flourishing the dagger.

Mintumi had had enough. '64646,' he said, and Betti, who had reclined in the settee, suddenly took a cell-phone from her pocket and made a call. 'Gogo, try this number' she said. '– 64646.' She waited, then – 'OK, do it.' She listened intently, and the lights in the room seemed to pulsate as Mintumi realised that, at that very moment, someone was bleeding his bank account of cash. And as the pastor of a church who had to be ready for all sorts of exigencies, the limit to each withdrawal was in the thousands of cedis. After about a minute Betti put the cell phone on the table. She turned to the pastor, and it seemed her mien was compassionate, and she said, 'Take the memory chip. If I were you, I would swallow it.' Mintumi had frozen in his seat, his eyes glazed. The others waited a while for Mintumi to recover. When nothing seemed to change and he sat there, statuesque, Betti spoke again, and her voice was full of concern. 'Won't you destroy the chip? Oh, we are not bad people, ooo, swallow it! Saman, help him swallow it. Asare, bring pastor some fruit juice.'

And in that manner, Mintumi was force fed the memory card from the camera. Mercifully, it was a micro-SD, and went down without much difficulty. 'Now you can go, Pastor,' Betti said. 'Thank you, you have been a sweet customer. If you want more, next week I will be at the same place, or if you like you can call me.' Betti placed a hand on Mintumi's cheek, stroked it in a motherly fashion, and then suddenly stood up and left the room.

But Mintumi could not follow her out, even though he tried to. This was because Saman restricted him, grabbing both of Mintumi's hands and twisting his arms behind him, transporting Mintumi thirty-five years into the past, into the hands of the primary school bully. 'You will leave by another exit,' Saman said. 'It is getting to morning. Do you want the girls in the compound to see you?' Asare had drifted to the back of the room, and Mintumi saw that there was a window there. But it was a small window.

'That window,' Saman said, following Mintumi's gaze, 'Is also known as the eye of the needle. You know what that means, don't you, sir?' His breath was hot on Mintumi's neck. 'The Kingdom of Heaven lies outside, and you must pass through the eye of the needle, impossible even for camels – but we will see what we can do! Look at your belt, designer belt. I'll take it. Look at your shoe. Designer shoe. I'll take it. Look at your watch. Designer watch. I'll take it.' And so under the spell of the dagger Mintumi was undressed again, standing once again in his boxer shorts. There were tears of desperation in his eyes.

'It is a small window,' Saman said to Mintumi. 'Can you pass through?' 'It will be hard – his chest is broad,' Asare said. 'Bring the anointing oil,' Saman said. The bottle of oil that Asare brought from the dresser, was, to Mintumi's horror, the all-too-familiar 'Jerusalem Holy Oil'. 'This is for lubrication,' Saman said, pouring the contents of the bottle on Mintumi's shoulders, and spreading the oil over his torso, his long fingers playing deftly on the skin – all done so swiftly that Mintumi could barely protest.

Then the two men helped him through the window, by holding his legs and feeding him, arms first, through the aperture. It was truly a tight fit about his shoulders, and the olive oil did in fact assist his egress. But as his chest popped through the window Mintumi felt the cold steel of the dagger against his waist, and he screamed, and kicked – and Saman drew the knife back, and cut off his boxer shorts.

CHAPTER 5, WHICH CONCERNS THE EVENTS THAT OCCURRED AFTER MINTUMI'S RELEASE.

Mintumi crashed into the dirt outside the window, breaking the fall with his hands and rolling to a stop against the wall. He had landed in an alley, stark naked, and the sky was lightening as dawn broke. He heard a shout of derision, and though it first sounded far away, it was in fact quite close. He turned and saw Saman's head framed in the small window. Saman was screaming with laughter. Then Saman's head disappeared and was replaced by Asare's head. Asare shouted, 'Pastor!' and then Asare's head disappeared and again Saman's head re-appeared, hooting with laughter. This was more than Mintumi could bear. 'Foolish shit!' he shouted back, 'Foolish!' and then he ran down the alley, and when he came to the end of the wall he crouched, and peered around it.

He was in a poor neighbourhood. The alley opened into an untarred road that meandered between the crooked walls of poverty-stricken houses weary of carrying their rusted roofing sheets. About twenty feet away in an open compound behind one of the houses, there was a drying line strung between two wooden pillars. Two lone pieces of clothing dangled in the keen morning breeze: a cream coloured shirt, and a pair of dark brown shorts. Mintumi sprinted into the yard, tore the shorts from the drying line and fled, taking refuge behind the wall again. Panting heavily, he prayed no one had seen him. In this neighbourhood, he was sure he would have been lynched without any questions. However, it did occur to him that being murdered was not a bad way out of his predicament and impending disgrace. But Mintumi resisted the thought! he was not ready to die. He was working to recover his dignity! Yet, as Mintumi struggled into the shorts it struck him that he had just stolen the school uniform of a J.S.S. student. The poor chap had probably only one set, and might have washed the clothes after school for use again the next morning.

Now that he was no longer naked Pastor Mintumi had more confidence. What a difference a piece of cloth made! And so Mintumi understood the need of Adam for the cover of leaves, after the fall, long ago in the Garden. True, he was barefoot, and only had on the shorts which were tight at the waist but opened up in a generous flow towards the knee. But these were not an ordinary pair of shorts, he surmised, these were the current incarnation of the venerable knickerbocker. Mintumi silently cursed the tailor on behalf of the innocent school boy as he crept along the wall, breaking into the open, into the street, and then crouching forward again. Mintumi had no idea where he was. Somewhere not too far away, his nice car, the Touareg, was waiting for him. But his keys were in the pocket of his trousers, and his trousers were in the custody of Saman. Therefore, it was no use, even to locate his car. And how about taking recourse to technology to avoid his bitter fate? True, he could have telephoned one of the more discreet members of the church, and tell him he had been waylaid and robbed. But his new Samsung smartphone was in the other pocket of his trousers, and his trousers were in the custody of Saman, and Mintumi's new-found hatred for Saman therefore knew no bounds. A police station, the natural, logical resort for an ordinary citizen hard done by in such a manner, was of course out of bounds to someone like Mintumi. A statement would have to be written! Investigations would commence! He was guilty of soliciting! The press would be involved! Ruin lay along that path! He could appeal to his fellow citizens for help. Some clothes to look presentable, some money for a taxi – to take him where? Home? How could he meet Millicent in this state? Mintumi was facing a crisis such as he had never faced before. And far in the deep recesses of his mind he worked out that, had Masgo been in his shoes, he would have breezed out of trouble without sweat. Perhaps, due to Masgo's correct application of the 'Jerusalem Holy Oil.'

East of course was the direction in which the sky was lightening, but since he was following the road, Mintumi had no real control over the direction in which he was headed, save a choice of forward or backward. The road seemed to go north-east, and Mintumi followed it. Even if he had wanted to go towards the west he could not, because the way was blocked by rows of houses and shops. To go in the other direction was to go towards the south-west, which, if the road persisted in the same direction meant he would end up at the beach. It all did not really matter, though, because Mintumi did not know where he was. It seemed strange to him now, that even though he had lived in this city for about twenty years, there were so many places he could not recognise. But in actual fact it was a large city, and his business rarely brought him to areas such as this. It was a shopping district in a very poor part of the city. It teetered at the edge of a slum. On the contrary, his church was in one of the suburbs – a rather plush residential area – and his house a mere ten minute drive from the church. This had the benefit of attracting people from poorer neighbourhoods, who could console themselves with going to church in a posh neighbourhood even if they could not afford to live there. On the other hand, the rich were happy to have a church close by, and could also be kind to the poor without much effort. Matthew 25. A good chapter, Mintumi thought, his mind rambling. He would have preached from it this week.

Pastor Mintumi tried to assess his location by reading the signboards in front of the shops, but there was nothing there that was of any help. 'Ask God Enterprise. P. O. Box 9, —'. 'Anointed Hands Hairdresser'. 'Vorcanisa. Ponping tyre'. Lotto kiosks painted in the colours of the national flag.

The city was stirring, slowly. Being a Sunday morning, most shops would not open. A tro-tro snuck past him, with only the driver in it.

Presently Mintumi reached a crossroads. He looked to the left, and looked to the right, but chose to continue forward because a little way ahead, past the junction, he saw the blue sign-board and rain shelter of a bus stop. And there was a small group of people there, waiting for a bus. He could ask for directions. He could get on a bus. Charter a taxi. And go where? If he went home, what would he say to the gate-man? To the house-boy? To his wife? Lies! That was all that he would have for them. Lies, lies, lies. As Mintumi drew closer to the bus-stop he noticed that the people cast wary glances in his direction – in the direction of the man wearing a funny pair of shorts, walking in fits and starts, and looking around as if he had just been created and placed right there. The stares made Mintumi stop a little distance away – what would they do if he got closer? After a few minutes Mintumi saw a smallish man approaching at a fast pace. He was dressed in a pair of dirty jeans and a blue batakari, his face partially obstructed by the brim of a flat cap pulled forward. The man cast a nonchalant eye in his direction but otherwise paid no attention to him. When he got closer Mintumi raised a hand and said, 'Excuse me.' The man stopped, and there was no surprise on his face. 'Yes?' he asked. Mintumi said in a terse undertone, 'Please tell me where we are?' And the man looked with pity at Mintumi, and in the course of the exchange of a few words Mintumi discovered his bearings. It turned out that his church was not too far off, and were he to keep walking straight in an easterly direction across two main roads, he would be in the neighbourhood of his church. However, the subsequent behaviour of the man put Mintumi in grave doubt about the veracity of this information, and the subsequent behaviour of the man was as follows: After acknowledging thanks from Mintumi with a curt nod, the man proceeded at a steady pace to the bus stop, where he stopped and gazed imperiously at the people there. He seemed to be scanning the face of each person. After a minute or two he seemed satisfied with what he had found. 'Youth!' he declared with some disdain, adding, 'Nkolaa nkoaa.' Then the man proceeded over the road, which he crossed sideways like a crab, moving in little jumps, his arms outspread and his head wobbling. When he got to the other side he made an about-face, and then returned across the road in the same manner. 'Hay-ja!' the man shouted. Mintumi was worried about these developments. How could he trust the directions given by such a man? Yet the man had seemed lucid enough, and therefore Mintumi decided to ignore his current activity of marching on the spot beside the road to the growing amusement of the bystanders. But Mintumi also saw an opportunity for further disguise, and in a final act of sheer robbery, he ran to the man, snatched his cap off and sped on down the road, raising a cheer and applause from the growing crowd. The mirth generated was great indeed: see Mintumi half-naked, fitting the cap over his head as he ran, and the other man marching without a pause, regardless of the loss of his cap.

CHAPTER 6, WHICH CONCERNS MINTUMI'S DRAMATIC ENTRY INTO HIS OWN CHURCH, AND HOW THE STORY ENDS.

It took Mintumi over one hour of walking before familiar buildings began to present themselves. His feet were sore and blistered. He found himself gravitating towards the vicinity of his church, and each step took him closer and closer, it would seem, to an inescapable destiny, a golgotha.

Was it the force of habit, or was it because there really was nowhere else to turn, that caused Mintumi finally to make his way to his church? It no longer came to his mind, the thought that he could go home, or to a friend's, or to his sister's, or seek refuge until he could make himself presentable and prepare a coherent story. When earlier he considered such options, he faltered at the monumental lies that had to be crafted to buttress any narrative. Yet what lie could supersede the lie his life had been over the past years?

In any case, Mintumi's cognitive capabilities had collapsed almost everywhere, and only focused about the church, which was after all, his life's work. He was almost a motor-man, driven by basic emotion and reflex.

He passed beside the giant billboard declaring "Latter Days Prophetic and Evangelistic Ministry: We Preach Christ", featuring a full-length picture of himself in a sharp three-piece suit, with hand upraised. About a hundred feet further and he came to the entrance to the walled compound of the church. Attendance seemed to be very good, the car park was full, and as was usual, there were no loiterers about. Even before he staggered through the car park, Mintumi could hear the singing coming from the church. It was time for praises and worship, and the faithful were singing at full throttle, with the church band blasting away with cymbals and trumpets and guitars. The guy at the keyboard was phenomenal, as always. Inside the church, Mintumi knew, the congregation would be dancing, handkerchiefs aloft. Yet all could not be well in the church, since he, Mintumi, was supposed to preach the sermon this morning. Could he manage it, after all this, and in his state? Granted that he was ill-prepared, but as a preacher of many years standing he could pull a sermon out of thin air! – why, had God not so loved the world (John 3:16)? Did the thief not come to steal, kill, and destroy (John 10:10)? And was it not time to remind the church of the events of the end-times (Matthew 25)? Could he then enter the church, mount the pulpit, and preach? The forces against his pulling such a feat off were great. His state of undress could be excused, were one to stretch it – examples from the Bible and from history could be found – and in any case he could get a robe from the church offices, adjacent to the chapel. But his great awareness of his sin, the monstrous bearing on his conscience, these he could not overcome in a short while.

The music poured forth from the windows and doors, bathing Mintumi in sound as he passed the rows of cars, heading towards the doors at the side of the chapel. He could see the riot of colour as the congregation danced away inside – But where would Millicent be? Usually, as osofo yere, Millicent sat beside him in the front row, along with the other pastors and the deacons. Would she then be sitting there, alone? Would she have come to church at all? Or would she perhaps be at the police station, making a report about her missing preacher husband? And the children, where would they be in the congregation?

The very rafters were shaking with songs of praise as Mintumi staggered into the chapel, the shock of his presence having transformed the usherettes at the entrance into temporary statues, a few of whom nevertheless released ear-shattering screams. He gained entry unimpeded and advanced at a rapid pace up the aisle, towards the podium. The commotion caused by the appearance of the founder and head pastor of the church, dishevelled, bare-chested, bare-footed, clad only in poorly-fitting knickerbockers and a flat cap, had brought the service to a standstill. The band had stopped playing and an unholy hush rapidly replaced the shouts made in shock and the hubbub born of consternation and confusion. Mintumi almost made it to the podium before he suddenly collapsed and lay twitching on the floor. Millicent was in church. She had come along with their children. She had not been unduly perturbed about her husband's absence from home, because she thought that he might have been taken up with the work of the Lord, somewhere in town, and she had seen no reason to change the usual Sunday routine. But, since she was sitting in front, she had a close view of Mintumi's sudden appearance, and as he fell she rose, hand to her mouth, too shocked to scream, and then collapsed backwards into the chair which tipped over and crashed to the floor. But no one paid any attention to her, as they pressed towards the place where Mintumi lay. The junior pastor, who had been presiding in Mintumi's absence, stepped forward in amazement at this latest feat of Satan, and as he approached the felled pastor the congregation began to form a circle around Mintumi, who lay on the floor in a rather unnatural pose, his right arm outstretched and his left hand under his torso, his knees huddled together. The pastor paused for a moment at this awful sight. He had no idea what had happened, but this was clearly a manifestation of some terrible, terrible, evil, and there was only one thing to do. He stretched forth his hand. 'In the name of Jesus,' he begun, 'we come against this demonic attack.' The silence that followed this statement was charged. The junior pastor raised both hands. 'Brothers and sisters,' he began, 'This is spiritual warfare! If you are not strong in the spirit, step back. Let the prayer warriors step forward.' An inner circle of men and women soon formed, while the rest of the congregation milled around the prayer warriors. The pastor led the charge. The passion of the prayers was so intense that the entire congregation was whipped into a frenzy of glossolalia, and the very foundations of the building trembled with feet stamping and the windowpanes vibrated with hand clapping and the church resonated with shouts. Mintumi revived momentarily –

–   opening his eyes he saw a forest of outstretched hands partially obscuring the light from the fluorescent lamp directly overhead, and he could see his junior pastor trembling all over with the intensity of his prayer –

–   he wondered if his children were also there, praying –

–   and before he passed out again he saw the thick lips of Masgo shouting the name of the Lord.

THE GONJON PIN

Yᴏᴜ ᴅᴏɴ'ᴛ ᴋɴᴏᴡ Billy Holmes, do you? Of course not. Not personally, anyway, which is what I really meant. In any case, I am not going to introduce him to you. However, something happened to him which affected one of my friends, and that is the story I want to tell. Billy is not his real name, though. It's his writer's pseudonym, under which disguise he has displayed the most wretched behaviour known in publishing.

What I want to tell you about Billy is that, one fine day in late July, when the weather in Accra is quite mild and an evening walk refreshing, this man leapt over the balcony of his first-floor apartment in East Legon and fled screaming down Sergeant Adjetey Street, pursued by no-one. He was stark naked, and ran in the direction of the open-air restaurant at the end of the road, where early revellers were provided with an enhanced visual experience. This event was captured by several persons on their devices and the video is now online.

He ran 200 feet in all before he was reached by the 'first responders', ever-concerned Ghanaians who wanted to help but also wanted the inside story – the scoop – and they reported that his first words upon being accosted, at which time he also must have come to his senses, were: 'Oh, what a shit.'

His story, in sum, was this. He was enjoying early evening entertainments after a good supper – fufu and antelope light soup, no less – when two women came to his house and offered themselves to him. Of course, he was not entirely crazy, he was acquainted with at least one of them; yes, she was his friend – indeed, an ex-girlfriend, and they had parted on good terms etc, let me not spoil the story. In any case Billy was entirely amenable to these suggestions, but unfortunately the other woman turned out to have balls and proceeded to beat Billy while his former girlfriend laughed and fire came out of her mouth – and so he had no choice but to flee, naked though he was. In order to follow this interesting lead to the end, the concerned Ghanaians, after preserving Billy's dignity with a donated shirt, went to his apartment where they discovered nothing to confirm this story, with the exception of ruffled bedclothes, which really proved nothing. In the end Billy was advised to relax, to go to the police if he was worried, and to stop smoking 'the thing'. 'The thing', the man who proffered this advice said, could disgrace even the mightiest. I assume he alluded to a psychotropic substance.

Be that as it may, disgrace – induced by psychotropic substances or otherwise – was Billy's stock in trade. He published a one-man online and print tabloid, issued twice a month, titled and captioned, respectively, The (Scurrilous) Rag – No Smoke Without Fire. Oh, what obscenities had he not published! What reputations had he not destroyed! Politicians brought down! Public officers disgraced!

Marriages ruined! Secretly recorded sex videos! Occult practices of the rich and famous! Of course, all this meant that his website received hundreds of thousands of weekly hits, his newspaper was widely circulated and read, and he was hated by a few, and loved by few. Nevertheless, his business paid off, and he was rich. As the event which I have recounted happened only last week, I wait to see what the next edition of The Rag will publish.

But this is not really the story I want to tell. I want to tell you about what happened to my friend Kumi, who two years ago was kicked out of the University of Ghana, where he had been studying Computer Science and Philosophy. Kumi's apartment is on the same floor as Billy's. When you climb up the stairs to the landing, Kumi's apartment – A-1 – is to the left, and Billy's – A-2 – is to the right. So, you may ask: how did it happen that Kumi, whose background and family circumstances were as humble as my own, was the owner of this plush apartment in an upscale Accra neighbourhood, when he had not even completed university and was unemployed? This is an important part of the story, as you will see. Kumi had always had difficulties in school, even though he was a very bright student. He is a rather quiet chap, an introvert, in fact – a geek, if I may take the liberty – but his rebellious nature, on full display when he was forced to do things he considered unnecessary, meant that he had been dismissed from various schools and only entered the University because he passed his exams as a private candidate. So, though Kumi was my classmate in secondary school, I finished University three years ago, and now work as a radio journalist.

Kumi did not tell me why he was dismissed, but here is what I gleaned from one of his classmates. Apparently incensed by what he considered a misrepresentation of Kant's categorical imperative, Kumi had fallen into a heated argument with his professor during a lecture. What started off as a probing question from Kumi quickly turned into a curious spectacle. Kumi declared, the professor disagreed, Kumi insisted, the professor dismissed, and so Kumi rushed to the board to demonstrate a point, drawing circles and arrows on the board. The professor rejected the proposition, threw his jacket on the desk, and drew a diagram of his own. The three other students left the classroom as voices rose and tempers rose with them. The head of department, whose office was just down the hallway, was alarmed at the noise and rushed into the lecture room where he found the two sparring philosophers enveloped by a cloud of chalk dust, shouting at each other and drawing and erasing diagrams on the blackboard. The two did not take kindly to the head of department's interjection, with Kumi screaming that he was a 'dudui element'. And so he was dismissed, the University not taking kindly to such insulting behaviour. You may ask, yes, but how does that relate to the apartment? And the answer is this: a few months after his dismissal, Kumi won a quarter of a million cedis in the National Lottery.

After he moved into his new apartment, Kumi embarked upon a secret programme. Now, though I'm telling you the story, I have taken pains to conceal all identities, so it still is a secret programme, even though you know about it. It is still secret because it is so totally removed from your life that you cannot do anything about it, any more than you can do anything about Anokye. Or Babayaga.

I first visited Kumi in his apartment about six months after he moved in, on a calm Sunday afternoon that offered only the thrills of boredom. The weather in the city was gloomy from the threat of rain. There was this languorous air about the afternoon and, by the time I got off the bus to walk the one or so kilometres to Kumi's place, I was beginning to feel slightly depressed. The tree branches that overhung the pavement were dropping some tiny yellow flowers. I waited beside an old man for a sleek black Mercedes to roll by before crossing the road; he marched stiffly ahead of me, holding his umbrella like a sword.

Sergeant Adjetey Street, when I got to it, was deserted. A white Range Rover was parked outside the apartment block, but there was no one in it. I found Kumi in the garden, sitting at a round wooden table underneath a tamarind tree. He was poring over a chess board and looked very well indeed, sporting a handsome crew cut and a sprightly air. A few pawns and a bishop lay on their sides beside an ashtray. Smoke drifted upwards from a detritus of stubs.

'Finally, we meet again,' I said, dropping into a seat opposite him. 'This is where you've ended up.'

Kumi smiled, waved a hand lazily over the board, and said: 'In three moves the white king will be in check. In two additional moves the game will be over. The white king does not know this. And so the hand of fate deals with us all.' He picked up a piece, consulted a pamphlet on the table, and said, 'Black knight to E 6.' He moved the piece across the board.

'Pretty grand,' I said, looking up at the four-storey block, the white of the walls in stark contrast to the bright reds and greens of the flame trees blooming in the garden.

'Spirits upstairs,' Kumi said, rising. 'Come on in. I have something to show you.' I followed him up the stairs, noting that he had put on a little weight, so that he was no longer lanky. On the landing we turned into apartment A-1. 'Odd neighbour I have,' Kumi said, shutting the door behind him. 'Billy something. Has orgies and such. I hear he's a writer of some sort. Aspirational stuff for you, perhaps.' Despite the air-conditioning, the room was charged with cigarette smoke, and unshaded lights glared from the ceiling, reflecting dully from the pale green tiles of the bare floor. The room was bare save for two armchairs, a piano, and a bar to which I was steered.

'Let us imagine,' Kumi said, cracking open a Jack Daniel's and half-filling my glass, 'that a man could predict the future... no, let me put it better – imagine that a man could predict future events. Would that skew the temporal trajectory?'

'Spare me the philosophy,' I grumbled. 'It's all tosh anyway.'

Kumi laughed. 'Predetermination proscribes probabilities, or does it? You believe in God, of course.'

I finished my whiskey and reached for the bottle again. It was really good stuff, so it did not bother me that I drank it neat. 'You are not normal, clearly,' I said to Kumi, 'But do give it a shot sometimes. Show me around your place. Seems like you are putting it to shame.'

Kumi run a finger back and forth across the counter. 'You know how I won the lottery?' he asked. I looked at him. He hadn't told me about it, and no one else had either. 'A dead man, my friend. A date of death, the number on the motor hearse. Ten digits and the remainder of my student loan. I've since wondered how could that happen, when the odds were so great. Was it in fact because the odds were so great, or because of... the hand of fate? God?'

'Satan,' I put in drily. 'God does not play dice.'

'He plays chess,' Kumi said, striking up another light and handing me the pack of Rothman's. I declined. He released a stream of smoke in my direction. 'Let me show you around,' he said, and, grabbing the bottle, led the way into the next room. There was nothing in it, and it apparently had not been cleaned in a long while, so I wondered why he bothered to show it to me. 'One,' he said, swinging the door shut and sauntering off.

'There's this thing I want you to see,' he said, stopping suddenly beside a shut door and gesturing with the bottle. 'There's only a bed and a stereo in this room... and a bookshelf. Surely you've seen these before? They look just like any other. Good. Let's go on, then.' I noticed that his hand was trembling and his breath came a little more rapidly. I caught him casting a sideways glance in my direction, and he looked away self-consciously. We stopped again at another shut door.

'This is my study. And I am working on a project.'

There was a throbbing hum coming from the room, and, with an expression on his face reminiscent of a child saying to another, 'promise you won't laugh', he threw the door open.

A rushing noise – like the sound of an industrial air blower – leapt from the room like a tiger, making me step backward. The sound was coming from the right side of the room, where, against the wall, there was a row of shelves carrying what appeared to be the biggest computer workstations I had ever seen. There were ten of them, and each CPU was about three times the size of a desktop CPU. There were network switches too, with green and red lights blinking merrily. Cool air blasted from four air-conditioners on the opposite wall, and there was a table in the middle of the room with an open laptop computer on it. A blue swivel chair was placed a little way behind the table, beside which reclined a single armchair and a coffee table. Three or four large books lay on the floor beside the table. Against the wall behind the armchair there was a whiteboard with equations scrawled across it in blue ink.

'Goodness,' I said softly, looking around in awe. I walked slowly across the room to the window. Through the open blinds I saw the laden branches of a yoryee tree. I turned around and surveyed the room again.

Kumi's agitation was increasing, he seemed to be bouncing up and down – but I had also been drinking, you see, so my perception of small movements could have been suspect. He was speaking, but I only caught the words: '... improving the prediction capability of repeated random events from a finite p-space by a method of reduction. How does that sound? Heh? Heh?'

Setting the bottle on the table, he lit another cigarette and began pacing back and forth. I told him I did not understand what he was saying. He farted unconsciously and, as the sad smell grew about us, he explained that he was writing software for predicting chance events which nevertheless occurred regularly – for example, floods, wars, and lotto numbers.

I took a deep breath. 'So,' I asked, 'you are building a lotto machine?'

'More or less,' Kumi said. 'But the scope is not so pedestrian – or mercenary. It can be employed for very useful things in science and engineering. Are you not interested in how it works? Heh?'

Kumi stopped pacing and approached me rather aggressively, his forehead glistening in the bright fluorescent lighting. I drew backwards involuntarily.

'But really, think of it,' Kumi continued. 'What will next week's lotto numbers be? I cannot tell, but could I tell, perhaps with greater certainty, what the numbers will not be? What about saying that this week's lotto numbers will not be drawn next week? This is my concept of repeatability. The first step is to derive a probability function for repeatability, because with that you can minimize the sample space, thereby reducing the odds. See? I am now running a program that I wrote to mimic the wheel of fortune, generate a hundred thousand draws, then test my concept of repeatability...' here, he indicated the computers with a flourish of his right hand, leaving a trail of smoke. He sat down and leaned forward. 'Should be done in about a week. And if it works...' he began, snapped his fingers, sucked deeply at the cigarette so that the end flared up like the evil eye, and then sat there holding his breath, all puffed up and filled with smoke.

We looked at each other. His eyes started to water. The seconds ticked. The whole thing was stupefying, and I just looked at him, thinking perhaps he would start to levitate and then... something. Instead he pressed a finger on his right nostril and let flow a thick stream of grey smoke through the left, and then he gasped loudly, fell to the floor and lay there, taking great gulps of air. I suddenly felt a strong urge to shout abuse at Kumi, but all I could do was mutter: 'This is all nonsense. Just don't kill yourself.' To which he replied from the floor, weakly, 'Ahhhhh'. He seemed happy.

Now let me show you how Billy's story intersected with Kumi's. Again, I must indicate that I have no real interest in Billy's case, save for a journalistic curiosity. I have only told you about what happened to Billy because of what happened to Kumi subsequently.

Last Thursday, at 8.30pm, I received a call from Kumi.

'Something terrible has happened.' He was whispering and I could barely hear him. 'Could you come to my place at once?'

'Will you pay for the taxi?' I asked, on account of the persistent economic difficulties related to my profession.

'This is serious,' he sighed. 'Come at once.'

It was during my approach to his apartment that I met the aftermath of the commotion involving Billy. There was a small group of people talking and laughing at the entrance, so I asked them what was going on. They happily gave me details of Billy's mishap. Then I went up the stairs, and Kumi met me at the door.

He looked harassed, and asked, without preamble: 'Did you by any chance tell anyone about my... project?'

'Of course not,' I replied. 'I keep confidences. What's going on?'

'My study has been violated,' he said, a slight trembling in his voice. 'Someone broke in. And that is not all. Come.' He led me into his study. The window had been smashed to pieces, obviously by a concrete flower vase which now lay on the floor, spilling soil. A clutch of broken periwinkles had fallen just beside the window. Pieces of glass and soil lay scattered about the floor. The window was open and the blinds fluttered in the breeze.

'He came in via the balcony,' Kumi said.

'You saw him?' I asked.

Kumi shook his head. 'I was asleep. Was woken up by the crash. But there was no-one here when I came in.' Anticipating my next question, he said, 'No, nothing was taken. Nothing was touched. But...'

My eyes, led by his raised hand, followed his index finger past the table on which his laptop sat, past the shelves with the blinking servers and humming workstations, and stopped just behind the armchair, a little way to the left.

'What the hell is that?' I exclaimed.

'It's someone's balls,' Kumi said, in an apologetic tone. 'Someone's balls hanging on my wall.'

We approached the wall. The scrotum was gross to look at, with patchy brown corrugated skin and straggly hairs. The dash of talcum powder did not make things look any better.

'Oh God,' I said. Kumi could be cantankerous, but practical jokes were not his forte. This was no joke. At all. I stood there staring at the wall. I could think of nothing. Kumi was breathing heavily beside me.

'You know, it is alive,' he said suddenly, breaking into my blank spell. 'It responds to stimuli. Look,' and he struck out with his pencil. The scrotal sac contracted immediately, and in my mind I heard the owner's anguished scream. An evil look crossed Kumi's face as he struck the balls again.

'Stop that,' I said.

'What do you think is happening?' Kumi asked, his eyes fixed on the dangling mass. 'I tried pulling it off... but it's stuck, truly. Like it grew there.' His words made my stomach turn.

'What are you going to do?' I asked. Kumi shrugged.

At that time it had become clear to me that Kumi had no idea of what had happened earlier that evening involving his next-door neighbour. I had already begun to connect the dots. So perhaps Billy had not been hallucinating after all, and had really been attacked. I told Kumi what had befallen Billy.

'And so you think,' Kumi begun, 'that this chap attacks Billy, Billy jumps down and runs away, and then he comes here through the window. Why? To escape, or to... do the same to me?'

'Escape, most probably. This is not likely to be about you – you do not have enough enemies, Billy does. But Billy said that there were two of them, a man and a woman. Most likely they heard the crowd bringing Billy back into his apartment, so they rushed in here, hoping it was vacant, and then they heard you coming...'

'...and then they touched the wall and vanished. Except that the man left his balls behind. You know, that's a silly story.' Kumi said. He struck the balls again, rather absent-mindedly, and then began to pace.

The doorbell rang. It sounded far off, and must have been ringing for a while before we noticed it. Kumi went off and soon returned with a tall, burly man in a black suit. His round head was clean shaven and polished so that it shone under the fluorescent lighting, and he had a severe expression on his face, accentuated by a heavy – though well-clipped – moustache and beard that made his lips look like small animals in a forest. He had this nonchalant air about him, accentuated by the seriousness of his black bow-tie. He paused for a moment at the door and surveyed the room slowly, his right hand in his pocket.

'This is George,' Kumi said to me, and George spared me a nod. He looked like the MC of an awards event, plucked right off the stage.

'Are these the balls?' he asked, and bent to examine them. After a few seconds he straightened, turned, and walked to the window, carefully avoiding the debris on the floor. He gazed at the window without a word, and then came back towards us, paused at the whiteboard, picked up the eraser, and cleaned off Kumi's equations. Then he drew a large question mark followed by a line that travelled diagonally across the board, ending with an arrow head pointing at the offending scrotum.

'At this time, somewhere in Accra, or Ghana, there is a man walking about without balls. These are his balls.' George pointed. 'Let me tell you what has happened. This man – shall we call him "X" – has vanishing juju. This type of juju is quite well known. However, something must have gone wrong, and X vanished and left his balls behind.'

Kumi stared at George in stupefaction, his mouth hanging open.

'Do you expect me to believe this stupid...' He seemed lost for words, and it was a few seconds before he completed his sentence: '...shit? I am a rational man. Take a look around the room, there is science going on here, man! And you want me to believe... this...?'

'What?' George asked. 'It is right before your eyes, the balls. I do not ask you to believe it, I am offering you an explanation. It is very rational. Am I not making sense?'

'Not at all,' Kumi replied. 'What is "vanishing juju"? How can a man just vanish?'

'It is right before your eyes,' George said. He seemed to be getting annoyed, his eyebrows had dipped lower, and his mien was increasingly menacing. 'Call it what you will,' he said. 'You like science? Why is it not possible? Consider it in terms of quantum entanglement. A warp in spacetime. Science can always propose something.'

George turned back to the whiteboard. He made a list in large letters: '1 Call the police. 2 Alert the scientists. 3 Get the spiritualists. 4 Cut off the balls and throw them away. 5 Do nothing.'

'Cutting off the balls is out,' George said, and drew a line through the words. 'There will be bleeding, blood all over.

And X might perhaps die. That would be murder. Don't involve the police – this matter will enter into unimaginable absurdities if you do. Likewise the scientists, though I rather fancy that option. The police would get involved then, as well. Now to the spiritualists. But which? Do we go to Master Hindu or to Al-Zimbirigu? You see those adverts in the papers every day. But there's too much mumbo-jumbo and really they do not know what they are about – you don't think so? And now consider the last item, which is to do nothing. This seems best. X, seeing a patch of concrete wall where his testicles used to be, should be even more worried than you are. It's his problem mainly. He will solve it.' George put a big * beside item 5.

George's line of thought seemed quite reasonable to me, though I believed that the spiritualists should still be considered. Then maybe a juju man would have to be brought on site, fly whisk and bells and cowries and all, in which case, would the man have to come back to fetch his balls, or could he have them remotely returned? Despite the seriousness of the situation, a small laugh bounced about in my belly, but I did not let it out.

Kumi was standing behind me and I turned around to look at him. His face was creased in an angry frown and his Adam's apple worked up and down. I could see he wanted to talk, but it took him a little while to calm down sufficiently. When he finally spoke, his hands were trembling and his voice was hot with anger. 'Do nothing? Am I to live with someone's testicles hanging on my wall? Oh, the very thought!' Kumi shouted.

George looked at Kumi, his face expressionless. He raised his right hand and stroked his moustache. This seemed to infuriate Kumi further. 'I cannot stand this!' he shouted. 'Your premises are faulty. All your thinking can only lead to a wrong conclusion! There is a rational explanation for all this, we can understand it all without recourse to magic! That's right. There are no balls on the wall! It's just some sort of a mirage, a trick of the lights – or perhaps the periwinkles are exuding some hallucinogens... I cannot accept what you are saying!'

'Will you behave yourself?' George asked sternly. He was clearly out of patience and his jacket tightened across his chest as he flexed his muscles.

'Look, Kumi, take it easy or we'll just leave,' I said. I did not like the way things were going at all. Kumi had a wild look in his eyes and his breath was coming in short, loud bursts. He looked on the verge of a hysterical breakdown.

'Well, get out, then, get out! I'll take care of it myself!' Kumi shouted, and fell backwards into the armchair. 'Go!'

So we left, George and I, leaving Kumi fuming in the armchair with the balls dangling behind him.

'He's a peculiar sort of asshole,' George said to me as we went downstairs. 'But I'm sure he'll come around.'

There was a dark-grey Jaguar X8 parked on the street just outside the apartment block. George walked slowly to the car, got inside, and drove off. The bastard didn't even bother to give me a lift. I went home by bus.

Who was this George character? So well educated, well-dressed, rich, odd. Where was he from? I do not know. I'll ask Kumi, of course. It is an important item that I must include in the story. But all sorts of other events have since occurred, and as I sit here writing this I have still not asked Kumi about George. In any case, let me tell you what happened next, and you will see why I forgot to ask him.

Today is Saturday. Seven hours ago, at 11.40 in the morning, I received a call from Kumi. He did not bother with greetings.

'Oh God,' he groaned. There was a depressing weariness in his voice.

'Take it easy,' I said.

'I've been arrested by the police... They want to search my house.'

'Wait... The police? What happened?' 'This is not the time!' Kumi screamed.

'Then when is the goddamn time?' I shouted back. 'Give me some...'

'OK! OK! I threw the thing over the Adomi Bridge... and then there is this man behind me and he says we've got to talk... and he's a policeman... and I asked that you be there as witness... so we're coming to your place...'

'What? You're bringing the police here?' I was more amused than alarmed at this twist.

'We're outside your frigging door!' Kumi screamed.

I went outside. Kumi's Range Rover was just pulling up under the large neem tree outside my house. I live in a compound house at Adenta, and my neighbours, two of whom were playing draughts on their veranda, were staring at the resplendent item of luxury and casting glances in my direction as well. There was a man in the front passenger seat and as I stepped forward he got out and walked towards me. It was the policeman. He was in mufti, and well dressed at that. With his white shirt, rose-coloured flying tie, black trousers and leather shoes, he could have been a business executive. He held out his hand, stopping me in my tracks. I shook it.

'Detective Nketiah, Police CID,' he said. 'I believe you know Kumi S— ?'

'Is anything the matter?' I asked, looking at Kumi, who had placed his head on the steering wheel, the very picture of dejection.

'We have a standing warrant to search No 102 Sergeant Adjetey Street,' the detective replied.

I noticed that the detective's lips were unnaturally black, much darker than the rest of his face in fact. He went on: 'We've been monitoring a lot of suspicious activity there. I wanted to have a word with your friend at home – to ask him a few questions, informally, you see. He requested your presence. Shall we go right away? We may not need you for long.'

'Doesn't he need a lawyer?' I asked. 'He declined. This is informal, really. Just a few questions. But if he refuses, I'll arrest him and we'll have to go through the formalities at the station.'

The whole thing did not seem threatening, so I shrugged and said, 'Oh well. Let's go.' I was not doing anything serious at home and could spare the time. In any case I was really curious as to where this was going, and wanted to be part of the action. I went back inside, locked up, and returned to the car after about five minutes. Inspector Nketiah was still standing where I had left him, a little way from the car. He came up to me and whispered: 'But your friend, is he correct?'

'Most of the time.' I replied.

We got into the car. Kumi whispered a greeting to me in a cracked voice. He avoided looking at me, but I saw in the reflection in the driving mirror that his hair was uncombed and he was covered in grey dust. He was wearing the same clothes he had been wearing when he threw George and me out of his house. He smelled of sweat and tiredness.

I found out during the drive that Kumi had pretty much told the detective everything that had happened, and in the ensuing conversation I also got to know the circumstances of his arrest. He had been picked up a few minutes after throwing 'what appeared to be a heavy weight' over the railings of the Adomi Bridge. Though the action was not very suspicious in itself, Kumi's haggard looks and guilt-ridden demeanour made the detective pull him in. It turned out that Kumi had been tailed from his house – apparently, the police had put the apartment under surveillance. Perhaps Billy was involved in something shady, and the eyes of the law had turned in the direction of the occupants of No 102 Sergeant Adjetey Street. After days of struggling with himself about

what to do, Kumi, in a fit of suicidal desperation, had gone
and bought a hammer and a chisel and proceeded to remove
the section of the wall to which the balls were attached,
which he succeeded in doing after about three hours of work.
Exhausted, he had fallen asleep and woken up at dawn today.
Then, still covered with dirt and stone chippings, he had put
the thing into a bag, jumped into his car, and driven off to
dump it into the Volta.

When we arrived in Kumi's study I saw that there was
a hole the size of a football where the balls had been. It was
like an ugly scar in the smooth tan of the wall, with rough
and jagged edges. Loose chippings and dirt were strewn all
over the floor close to the wall. A large block hammer and a
concrete chisel had been tossed carelessly aside.

Kumi poured himself a large whiskey and lit a cigarette,
obviously in an attempt to calm his nerves. He sat in the
armchair, staring blankly at the computers that went on
running whatever program it was he had written, calculating
his 'prediction capability of repeated random events from a
finite p-space by a method of reduction'. Detective Nketiah
walked around the room, examining each item carefully
and writing things down in a small notebook. He asked few
questions – obviously the facts seemed to fit the story. Then
he sat down in the chair behind the table and asked Kumi
for a cigarette. It was at this time that I got the suspicion
that his unnaturally black lips were due to heavy smoking
of marijuana and tobacco. I had noticed this before in a few
other smokers. Besides, the way he handled the cigarette,
running his thumb lovingly along the length before putting
it into his mouth, made me even more convinced. Anyway,
Kumi had offered him an expensive brand, right from a
carved wooden case.

The detective smoked in silence, his left hand hanging
over the side of the chair. His eyes were closed and his face
expressionless. I stood leaning against the door post, while
Kumi sat in the armchair with his head in his hands. The

roar of the computers seemed to grow louder with every second. Nketiah smoked slowly and with relish, letting the ash drop on the floor, and for the next four or so minutes he did not open his eyes. But then he stopped smoking, pinched off the lit end of the cigarette, and dropped the stub on the floor. He brought his notebook and pencil from his pocket and scribbled something, tore the sheet out and placed it on the table, weighting it down with the lighter. Then he rose, looking intently first at me, and then at Kumi.

'You young men should be careful, you know,' he said. He turned to Kumi. 'I'm not going to take your statement, you're not under arrest... so far it all looks OK. Quite crazy, but not too much, so it's fine. I'll be on my way now. Good afternoon to you.'

Detective Nketiah paused when he got to the door, and he looked straight into my eyes. Then, thrusting his left hand into his pocket, he walked out. His footsteps receded down the hall, and I heard the front door open and shut.

Kumi remained where he was sitting, his head still in his hands. It sounded like he was crying.

I went over to the table and looked at the note the detective had left behind. There was a single telephone number on it, followed by the words: 'Call me if you get your machine to work. H. N.'

THE MAKING

WHEN HE GETS to the parking lot he finds that somebody has written in the dust covering the rear windshield, "Fucker".

There was a time in the past when this incident would have disturbed him greatly, moved him, perhaps, to anger. "Who is this ignorant fool?" he would have seethed, and perhaps tried to find said ignorant fool and dealt with him. Or her. Except he was sure it was a man; a woman would do things more delicately perhaps, even if more maliciously. But it would have been difficult in those times to have written anything in dust covering his car, for his car, then a silver Opel Zafira, was kept spick and span, clean and gleaming, rain or shine, harmattan or not. In those times he was, in general, much concerned with his grooming.

I put it to you that Dongla has changed since the epoch of the Zafira we have spoken about, changed in a direction that has culminated in the fact that today he does not seem to mind that there was something written on the back of his Mercedes. Was the change incremental, or was it instantaneous? And also it remains to be answered, the question why, why? Why suddenly this boring non-reaction, that one cannot even make a story about? Nevertheless, we can try. Why, indeed, has Dongla paused behind his car, read and re-read the word, and even now lifts, as I speak, his left foot to proceed away, without a noticeable reaction? It is as if this is normal, a daily occurrence perhaps, to have words scrawled all over his car – or he has done it himself. Yet even then!

We may propose different reasons for this apparent change in Dongla's attitude. We might of course start with economics, but then, his cannot be the case of a man who has fallen on bad times and perhaps become poor after being rich. No. If anything, Dongla is wealthier now than he used to be. As I said just a while ago, he used to drive an Opel Zafira, but now drives a Mercedes M-Class, and owns a number of houses in the city. Amongst his favourite digs can be counted a mansion in East Legon. However, despite Dongla's wealth and relatively elevated position in society, which one would have thought would come with vanity expressed in various forms including unnatural cleanliness, his year-old M-Class is heavily coated with dust from the severe harmattan and has not been washed for at least a week. Which creates an additional difficulty in the telling, why has his car not been cleaned for a week? Obviously all these things are linked. They have to be.

Dongla is now much calmer in his response to such incidents. Clearly the times of an angry response to such unwarranted acts of vandalism are gone. Yet far be it from me to suggest that his animal spirits have diminished, truth be told they are only slightly reduced from the levels at which they were when he drove the Zafira to a smoky death, steam pouring out of the engine and oil pooling underneath the chassis, just as in times past a man would ride a horse to its death on some quest or other.

Could it be perhaps that age is beginning to tell on Dongla's character? It could, but I believe that to be quite unlikely, as a sole agent of this change. For, why would the passage of few years, a few trips on terra around old solis, a small advancement of the biological clock, a little more hardening of the arteries, a slight weakening in the sphincter muscles, why would this make his response so different from what would be expected? I daresay it is not due to age.

Could his indifference to the word, the writing of which was executed in florid letters with an underline for emphasis, be perhaps the result of an emotional crisis of some sort? Family troubles, maybe? Has his son, being of cantankerous bent, had another scrape with the law? Is he weighed down by the fact of his ageing mother failing under the onslaught of arthritis? I doubt this. His mother's health has been failing for ages, and she has an uncanny acumen for narrowly dodging the swinging scythe of the grim reaper, who only managed to snip off little bits of her, but not enough to kill. Oh, just some surgery to remove a length of perforated intestine. A procedure to drain fluid from the lungs. Constant medication to thin the blood, to manage the blood pressure, to control the stomach bugs which were getting a bit risqué, as if they could not wait for the death of the host organism. An orthopaedic bed to manage the creaking bones. And on the other hand Dongla's son is really not that bad, just rather boisterous, a chip off the old block really, so it is not that, not that. One might then reasonably begin to imagine that this demure reaction is the result of an emotional upheaval related to a romantic relationship with a woman. Cherchez la femme, eh? But this is not the case. He is in fact dating a ravishing woman of class and high social standing, the relationship is deeply satisfying to both parties, and indeed he is headed to her apartment tonight. They have been together for many years, going even beyond the epoch of the Zafira. It is obviously a testament to his good taste and natural prescience that he had been attracted to a woman whose beauty did not seem to fade. Afia is tall and well-proportioned, with long legs that escaped the horror of thinning at the calves. I note some other features, for example, the smooth curve of eyebrow that imposes a mesmeric state on those who focused too long. The large eyes with dark brown irises and veritable black holes of pupils. The smallish nose without a hint of fat at the nostrils. The full lips that offer the correct definition for luscious. The smooth skin with a solid brown tone. Of course gravity is attacking her buttocks; because they are generous, one can not expect otherwise, but the cheeks are holding their own quite well and it will be many more years before the flab. Until then. The breasts also show a remarkable tenacity and maintain a powerful bounce. Even without a bra they stand proud, and it will be many more years before the sag. Until then. So it is not as if he has become unhappy or disinterested in life, on account of a woman. Indeed, it would be out of place to even suggest that he has become unhappy or disinterested in life. His deadpan expression is rather typical, he is not given to wearing his heart on his sleeve, but in the past flashes of high emotion were not uncommon.

What about his health, you may ask? Well, his health! Let me get to the point directly and not vacillate in speaking about his liver, kidneys, heart, lungs, colon, prostrate, and so on – obviously you are a busy person and I cannot just take your time like that, the story must be short, striking, so yes! to the point. His sexual health is excellent. His erections are classic. His technique is flawless. His stamina is notable. His performance is applauded. He has no need for pharmaceutical or herbal assistance. He has spurned Viagra, the saviour of many of his contemporaries. A few of them have even died of heart attacks after nights on Viagra between the sheets. They, he thought, when he heard of their sudden demise, were fuckers. In every sense of the word.

Nor has he changed because of a religious conviction. An atheist since his youth, he is even more of a sceptic now. And it had been bad enough before, bad enough for the Monsignor – head of the Catholic School where he had taken his 'A' levels – it had been bad enough for the Monsignor to write on his report card "The young man seems to have a deep-seated irreverence for things Holy and of God, and shows a tendency to be derelict of the sacraments." Dongla's father showed this to him, and Dongla was secretly proud of it, and his heart was warmed, but little did he know it was just Satan stoking up the fires of hell in anticipation of the future reception, but I must not deviate from the core of the telling. Indeed, Dongla recently moved a charismatic pastor to tears with an open challenge related to the eating of the church tithes. In reply the mortified cleric had said shakily, "May the Lord God almighty who is hanging in the sky – (here I have translated from the Twi) – have mercy on you". No doubt, Dongla remains the hardened sceptic as he pauses to examine the word on the back windscreen of his Mercedes. The cross-bar of the F is furnished with a little twirl at both ends and the k has its right leg extending below the other letters, winding in a tight spiral.

We do of course have to consider some biological functions common to man, which in Victorian times were the subject of great euphemism, but now, now, in this twenty-first century replete with the acceptance of great abominations and utterly permissive of all words, we still regretfully have to put it this way, that the possibility ought to be considered, that Dongla desperately needed to ease himself. As is well known, persons sorely pressed with a bolus at the very end of the canal have been known to act extremely calmly, lest a passionate or reckless exertion brings about the disgrace. With regards to doing a number one, I hasten to point out that Dongla is not prudish at all, and would, even with minimal camouflage, without hesitation unzip, and let go. For number two he would have first sought out a bush, he hadn't been to secondary school for nothing.

All this is irrelevant though, since the office block behind him, all ten stories of it, is replete with modern amenities, all available to him. Only a masochist would hold such a need for so long, and furthermore, Dongla's drive home required at least one half-hour in traffic. Dongla is not a masochist. Thus, we have to disregard this consideration.

There was a time that he would have been bothered by the fact that the miscreant had written "Fucker", which was rather meaningless as it stood. It was not even an insult. Had he written, for it was a he rather than a she, had they written, "You fucker", it might have been more direct. In fact, in order to place the insult properly, the fool might as well have written, "Dongla, you fucker". And even gone on, in smaller letters, to describe the reasons for the statement. There was enough space on the glass, to be sure. But Dongla is this afternoon apparently unmoved. And why is Dongla, in this instance, unmoved?

One might be a little concerned that the incident earlier on in the day where a subordinate had played the fool with Dongla's name could have dampened his spirits. Nothing could be further from the truth, for he had suffered worse tomfoolery on account of his name, and even then, from a vulnerable position. And so why would he now be disturbed by such an incident when he was the powerful chairman of the board who could get a person fired with a simple raised eyebrow? To expand on this issue of his name, which, in full, was Dongla Kosi Kuma Kpesese Blessed, there are a few anecdotes that are worth a mention. Here is one. On a Friday night a few years ago, some time just after midnight, he was located in a nightclub near Labadi in the company of a voodoo chick who was excellent company and of delectable bodily proportions to boot. She was not his girlfriend but a regular consort who had dealings with the sinister, the shady, and the spooky. She introduced Dongla to Daryl, an American economist with the World Bank who also happened to be a sexually reckless CIA agent. On hearing the name the man burst into uncontrollable laughter and spilled his drink. For reasons not entirely unrelated to alcohol and designer psychedelics, he screamed "Dongler!" and laughed like one deranged. Dongla took this misbehaviour in his stride, and the two men struck up a tolerable acquaintance. Daryl immediately went on to show his linguistic prowess after explaining to Dongla that a dongler was a penis, usually of notable size, and going on tell him how he had learned earlier in the evening that the poor devils who had no choice but to fuck prostitutes on their feet in dark corners called the thing gyina ho gye. On the heels of which Vanessa the voodoo chick murmured irreverently "stand-do is good for you". Daryl, in a veritable paroxysm, screamed "Toto is good for boys and girls!" To conclude on Daryl, just so you know that justice happens in the long run, I mention in passing that he was soon removed from Accra to Acapulco and there shot dead within a week. Now, I have strayed a little in the telling here but I believe we can conclude that with such past experiences Dongla's indifference to the word written on his car was not related to the abuse of his name.

We could wonder if Dongla might be considering a matter of such gravity that he is not properly sensible to his surroundings. Philosophical problems have been known to cause such behaviour, one recalls the case of Archimedes, reported to have leapt naked out of a tub and ran bare into the street, and even that over a matter as small as the flotation of objects. More contemporary cases abound, some reaching the level of boring cliché, but Dongla himself could call to mind one such case, being that of the venerable Prof N —, renowned Ghanaian Professor of Mechanical Engineering, emeritus of the K— University, whose mind, in his waning years, was so greatly exercised with the problem of inventing a fufu-pounding machine that he had once sat staring at his dinner plate for hours and daybreak found him still at table, eyes glazed over the mental exertion. Dongla, when he heard about the case, was filled with sympathy. A fufu-pounding machine! O the complexity! Even how to control the eccentric motion of the mortar and minimize vibrations, especially of the harmonic sort. Such problems were known even in rocket engineering.

But Dongla is not thinking about philosophy, nor science.

The fact of the matter is that he's not sure what exactly is happening to him, and he passes each day more and more bemused.

One night, just about a month earlier, Dongla, fully conscious of the fact that life had treated him kindly, and that fate had strewn flowers across his path, had gone to bed fully satisfied and without a care in the world. Then he had a terrible dream. As dreams go, the content was rather mild, but he had not recovered since he woke up the next morning and found that the front door was open a crack, and a spider web linked the knob to the jamb. He dreamt that he had come home in the early evening as usual, and just as he reached out to open the door a large black dog with glistening fur and slavering mouth suddenly burst out of the house, ran down the steps and across the garden and leapt over the five-foot wall in one bound. To make matters worse, the stereo in the living room suddenly boomed, and Dolly Parton's *Jolene* started playing at a ridiculous speed. The noise was rapidly inducing insanity, and the stupid machine wouldn't stop when he pressed the button, it would not stop even when he pulled the plug, and it was only when he gave a kick that the bedclothes arrested his movement and he woke up, sweating. Then he went to the living room and discovered the slightly open door. But nothing in the house seemed to have been touched. After several telephone calls he convinced himself that no-one was playing a prank on him, and put the incident down to somnambulism – something which had never happened to him before – or perhaps false remembering about the night before. Maybe he had just not shut the door properly, and had had a bad dream too.

But when he sat down to breakfast, little things happened which unsettled him even more. Reaching for cream for his coffee, he found that the crockery inched away and stayed just out of reach. With a sudden movement he captured the naughty bit of china while also struggling to bring his mind under control, and poured with a shaky hand. In his cup the words slowly formed, stark white against the black, black, coffee:

"HERE IS MY STING."

"Death".

And for the first time in his life he drank whiskey in the morning. He drank enough to knock himself out, and lay in stupor the entire day. By evening the effects of the alcohol were wearing off, and when he got back on his feet things seemed back to normal.

But the fact of the matter is that he had no idea what was happening to him, and he passed each day more and more bemused.

*

And now Dongla smiles! even if thinly! A little sparkle lights up his eyes as he opens the back door, sets his briefcase inside, gets into the driver's seat and starts the engine. Seen in the driving mirror the word maintains its integrity.

Fucker.

Dongla puts the car in reverse and presses gently on the accelerator.

RAIN

It had been raining for hours on end. What had started as a welcome drizzle cooling the tropical afternoon had soon developed into a nasty storm promising floods and a slot on BBC news. Countless Africans doomed to a watery grave due to poor drainage and climate change.

Fenyi and Horla sat in the corner just across the counter where Jake, the barman, was mixing mind-numbing cocktails with delicate names like Evening Jacaranda.

Everybody loved Jake because he owned the place and allowed smoking everywhere, so it was really a comfortable hideout for Fenyi and his friends – even though Kwenne preferred bitters over cocktails.

Banahene had just joined the group, and was taking a trial puff at a cigarette. His incendiary success allowed him to begin speaking.

"Dana's dead." he said, reaching for the beer that Jake had caused to materialise on the table. "Must have taken the wrong turn, met the wrong people, said the wrong things." The level of beer in the bottle dropped alarmingly. "Biff! Baff! Beaten to death. Body found in an alley this morning."

All this with such an even tenor that he could have been discussing how to slice bread.

Horla began to sniffle.

"Do you think he'll go to hell? Will he go to hell?"

Banahene lit another fag.

"Yes," he said emphatically.

Horla burst into tears.

"Guy was screwing other people's wives. Was his stock in trade. And a bloody crook to boot. Yes, it's the fire all right." Banahene nodded, directing a stream of grey towards Horla.

Fenyi wanted to tell Banahene to go easy on Horla. Chap was just a kid really – sheltered life and all that. Had to be introduced to the facts of life gently. In any case, Banahene was being unnecessarily irreverent – after all, only last week Dana was boozing with them at this very table.

"You have to learn how to accord the dead body the proper disrespect – it's a cadaver, after all. Two things you must respect – the memory of the one who is dead, and death himself."

"Herself." Kwenne chipped in, a sarcastic smile making his face look crooked.

"Themselves," Fenyi said and Banahene spluttered into his glass. "Why do we think of death as a singular entity? The world may be replete with Deaths – each specialised in a kind of passing."

"Death does not describe an entity, it describes the phenomena. Even if caused by a million different entities."

Lightning flooded the room with a savage silver that made the skin tingle, followed by the most gargantuan and merciless thunder blast, which rattled crockery so badly that Fenyi, cowering under the aural assault, expected the world to end at once.

Fenyi had always feared that he would die while engaged in some trite activity – travelling to attend a funeral, for example. Or have a heart attack in the bathroom. Death was bad enough – when he died, he wanted the occasion to be grand. Blaze of glory, make the prime time news.

Death! To understand life one had first to understand the place of death. Fenyi suddenly felt a thrill – the surreal ambience of the pub must have had something to do with all this, he thought – yet the truth was there, there! The meaning of the cosmos was being revealed...

Some great truth was heaving untidily at the limits of his consciousness – if he could only name it! That would fix it! If he could only see it! Then he could name it. If he could only conceptualise... but big words broke the homing strength and he was way off the scent again and the thing heaving at the edge of his consciousness remained nebulous.

The glasses on the table trembled in resonance with another blast of thunder. Then the door caved in under a wall of water and the end of the world began.

BACK TO THE HALLS

She knew she had to run.

Through the large hall that stretched all around like an arena, underneath the ceiling — a coloured, patterned vault arcing an eternity away, she ran. And the light and shadows raced with her past the pillars and pillars and pillars around the hall, and the floor gleamed and reflected the dancing brilliance flowing from the windows that were like doors, flowing from the blaze of green and yellow, warm from the garden outside, this garden surrounding the entire hall.

Thrilling birdsong shattered the silence and yet the thrilling birdsong enhanced the silence. And she, lithe across the shimmering marble of the floor; her gait was sure, each footfall light, and as she flowed in her steps, the run was a dance.

She had never seen a living soul in the halls before, neither in this hall nor any of the others. She was the sole inhabitant, the only one who enjoyed the luxurious rooms, the magic of the table already laid, the bowls of fruit, and spiced roast pork, and jars of milk, and bread, and wine, the chair drawn back, it was for her and no one else. Because no other person lived in the magnificent halls. No one at all.

So she reached the open doorway and the garden without grew into encompassing blossom. She came through the portal, passing underneath a carved mahogany doorpost where trumpet-bearing seraphs delighted in an ebony universe.

The mid-morning sun was majestic in clear skies and the sprightly breeze made the blooms dip and bow and bob in gentle waves flowing across the paved garden paths. Roses bordered the fresh green rectangles of the lawns, throwing up reds, yellows and whites in challenge to the banks of sunflower, amber petals surrounding dark brown irises playfully observing the jacaranda in full blue bloom.

Fountainheads let go of sparkling jets, droplets breaking the light into a thousand pieces, and refracted arcs of colour danced just above the ponds.

And sweeping from shrub to tree to flower-bush, birds! Feathered and in flight, feathered and preening, throwing up all the colours of the rainbow and every hue that mellowed the spaces in-between, and as the birdsong rose in a chorus of chirrups and coo-coos above the tinkling flow of water, it became clear to her again, that here too, there was no one at all.

And she remembered him, that night, was it last night, as he leaned over and his face came close to hers, she thought he was going to kiss her...

But she knew she had to run. And her feet flew over the demure greys of the paved paths, and the morning air was crisp.

To sit under one of the trees and read would be heaven – to sit under the flaming flamboyant and hear him speak would be heaven. But he never came in the daytime, he came only at night, like a thief in the night: and his voice was a dreamy murmur.

By the time she reached the edge of the garden she was tired and she walked – slowly. For the garden was of great extent. It was octagonal in shape, and the hall, also octagonal, lay right in the middle of it. The garden was bordered on one of its eight sides by an eight foot concrete wall, and on the other seven sides by verdant greenery: here lawns with dwarf-wall borders, here hedges.

There were eight Halls, and each one of them was identical to the others, though not absolutely, so that it was possible for her to tell which one of the halls she was in. Placed at the corners of an octagon, each hall stood, separated by thirty-two thousand footsteps, they stood, huge, magnificent and empty every time that she visited them.

The wall ran parallel to a dirt road. The motorcars that ran along that road raised billows of dust, and the wall stopped the dust from blowing into the garden. The surface of the road had been churned to a fine powder. She went past the wall, onto the road – and then in dismay, gathered up the folds of her blue silk skirt as her shoes sank into the dust. But she walked on because she remembered, that night, one night...

She knew she had to find him. Far down the road, when she had left the Hall a long way behind, she came across a black motor hearse pulled up beside the road. The vehicle was coated with red dust, the dust had caked around the fenders, the bonnet was smudged with oil, and one of the wheel caps had fallen off. The engine was idling, rumbling in a slow rhythm as the crankshaft turned over, and over, and over, and again. A man was sitting inside the cab. There was another man urinating into the dust-coated grass growing beside the road. The man in the car looked half-asleep, he gazed lazily at her as she passed. One look at him was enough to show that he was not the one she sought. And how about the other... No, never, never. He turned, zipping up. There was a cigarette stuck in the corner of his mouth. He did not move as she passed without a word and paused at the back compartment. There she peered through the dust-coated glass, through the gap in the parted curtains. And she saw, reflected poorly in the window, the man approaching behind her, having done peeing. *'Why seek ye the living amongst the dead?'* he asked. She did not turn around. *'He is not here,'* he continued, and the smell of the cigarette smoke wafted through the air. So she moved on, not looking at the man. There was nothing that mattered. She remembered, she remembered the nights; it seemed to her that there was much unfinished business, too many gaps in the story... but she knew she had to find him. 'Lady! Queen of the Halls!' the man said. Thus addressed, she turned to face him. He was now standing beside the hearse. He had crossed his legs, and his body was at an angle to the vertical, surely he would have fallen had he not supported himself by placing his left hand on the body of the motor car. The cigarette, still smoking, was in his other hand. 'Lady! Queen of the Halls! Why do we never meet the other of the Halls, the man of the halls, your partner? Or does he likewise traipse the land elsewhere, at other halls, and you two never meet?'

Was there a man of the Halls? But he was there, last night, if it was last night and not the night before...

'Lady! When we drive the corpse – the coffin bounces in the back, and when speeding in the night, the dark night, the soul of the dead man creeps into the cabin, and says, easy on the bod, you know? easy on the bod. The bod is already late, can't get later. Go easy, go easy.' She said nothing, she stood stock-still. The man drew on the cigarette. From inside the cab the other man began to laugh. There was no reason for such nonsense, no time for such foolishness. And she was off, at a brisk pace. They did not know, how could they know, that last night, if it had been last night, he had played his fingers across her arms, her shoulders, all the time whispering a poem by that mad poet whose writing he adored, whispering into her left ear, the next night it would be the other mad poet into her right ear, and of poets and poetry he had an inexhaustible stock, but when he drew the flute the chills started from her shoulders and the tears came unbidden and the Universe lay at their feet. He blew magic into their lives and played the brilliance of unicorns riding across starlit nights and souls free to roam from star to star, and gentleness billowed in waves of perfume, like midnight glory, his night glory...

But one night, last night, his face had been so close, Kiss me, Kiss me, she gasped, and the magic broke and he was gone, and she had only the gaping emptiness till dawn rode into the sky with the coolness of the rising sun...

She had to find him.

A cloud of dust in the distance and the deep-throated groaning of an engine heralded the approach of a large vehicle, and soon it passed her an enormous machine, a steel behemoth, a man-made leviathan. It was carrying something heavy, something seen dimly through clouds of dust... Its big diesel engine was thumping, the ground was shaking, and the dust obliterated everything. She sent her mind forth to feel the steel muscle that strove under the steel sheath, the engine, bathed in hot oil, the pistons thumping away, the engine, hot and steaming and driving the great mass of metal forward... When the truck had passed dust settled in a fine rain, besmirching everything. Her clothes, cobalt-blue in the morning, had become a dusty red-brown. She was one colour all over. But she wouldn't turn back, she had to go on, on to the next Hall, and on to the next Hall, until she had been through all eight Halls...

Yet was it in his power to appear when he wished, or was he too, bound by this eight-fold way of caprice?

And if I could find you, I would come to you too, in the stillness of the night, I would be your succubus...

A stone bench cowered beside the road in the strengthening heat of the sun. There was no shade, but she was tired, tired, and she sat down, and shut her eyes. Come nightfall she would be in another Hall, and in the fragrances of the night, in her bathed freshness and sweet cleanness, in her perfumed seductiveness, would he come to her, murmuring poetry under his breath? She would move on to another hall, looking for him – but only in the octagon of the halls, her eight-sided universe with the halls at the vertices, and though there were no walls to keep her she could not leave that octagonal space. And she knew she had to find him, by herself, and then he would be real, be fixed, be there, for her...

It was clockwork perhaps – but the clock never wound down, no one ever broke free.

But she knew she had to find him.

ATTA

Were it possible to reach beyond the soulless ink scratched across the pages of these journals, to reach beyond the dry ink on yellowing paper which nevertheless tells the story of a man's life, were it at all possible to quicken these dry words, in what manner could it be achieved? For the dead know not anything, except that they might know that which is quite important to us in this investigation, they know what it is to die, and therefore perhaps could tell us, what the sum of all life is.

Dead at thirty-two years and four months, our subject, killed by the falling branch of a tree in a storm. How do we approach this study, having retrieved his journal, and carefully constructed a biography of our subject, Atta? We could ask him some questions, but could he tell us what we want to know? Would he speak to us? Even if we could raise his ghost, as some claim can be done, were we to raise his ghost, would it not talk rubbish? And why should we place any weight on words from a shade? And yet, Atta, you make a fascinating subject, and we shall proceed as if it could be done.

Atta, you dead at thirty-two years and four months, knocked down by the branch of a tree torn off by a fierce gale, smashed at the base of the skull and sent flying into a copse, it was only later, later, that we found out that it was you, Atta. What were you doing out in such a violent storm?

We have read your journal, we find it fascinating and we want to talk to you. There are many things we want to know, they disturb us as much as they seemed to disturb you. From your journal entries, you also wondered about that intangible thing always dancing at the periphery, that shifting shadow at dusk, hinting at something, the else, hinting, yet never becoming real.

Allow us to introduce ourselves, starting with the investigative panel. From the far right, seated close to the window, we have Gyamfuaa O., PhD Molecular Biology, Cambridge, next to her is Nana Osei K., PhD Gnosticism and Aysmptotic Divinity, Princeton, Freda B., M.D., PhD Forensic Medicine, Stonybrook, Beyema A., PhD Evolutionary Psychology, Yale, Moses A., PhD Analytical History, Oxford, and my good self, Vynta A., MSc Linguistics, Oxford. Our medium is Afrakoma T., PhD Anthropology, Stanford. Afrakoma is also an expert on totems and religious rituals of primitive peoples. We the members of this panel have known each other for many years, so there is a certain familiarity between us which I am sure you will forgive. Dr Osei is the recorder for this session. There are others on this research team who are not present here – we have three research assistants, all post-graduate students from the University of Ghana. This research is partly funded by the G— Foundation.

Atta? Did you speak? I did not quite catch that. "Damn?" is that what you said? No? Alright. Do not worry about the academic credentials of this panel. We have worked hard to make our questions non-technical and accessible to the lay-man. We have also vetted our questions beforehand for reasons of clarity and efficiency, though we might get carried away sometimes – that is only to be expected – but as soon as we notice such drifting we will rein in the questioning and return to the pre-set track. Again, as a result of the vetting there are certain questions which we will not ask you, for example, 'Have you seen God, or the Devil, are you in Heaven, or Hell, has there been a judgement, will there be one,' and so on. The reason for this is simple. We are fully convinced that religion is rubbish and God does not exist, so we will not bother. Ah, Atta, you have something to say? Speak, please.

– Well.

Well? Perhaps you wonder at this last? But why not, Atta. Why seek when you are already convinced of the answer? Why bother when your feelings tell you the truth? Ah, but surely Atta, you should admire the beauty of this epistemological model. It was perfected by gifted scholars who worked at it in America for several decades, finally achieving this most remarkable result.

In our investigations we discovered that you kept a journal from a very young age under avuncular instruction, but that you destroyed all your earlier journals when you turned 18, why did you destroy them? Well, even if you do not answer this question we do not mind. We have reconstructed those teenage years as well, Atta, and agree that your childhood should not be part of this conversation lest we succumb to temptation and commit Freudian abominations. In any case, we must thank you for leaving behind such a concise, well-written journal, with no dilly-dallying and beating about the bush and such like waste of time. Your writing was terse but detailed, your observations precise and to the point, you handled deep emotion without gushing, and had we met you alive we surely would have liked you much.

You seem to be our kind of man. Moreover, we all admit that your descriptions of sex are illuminating, we see the humour in your writing even though you did not lean towards the titillating. We shall exclude a detailed discussion of those intimacies on account of such experiences are rather common and we do not wish to be trite, but we intend to return to this matter later. Do pardon us if our questions seem rather disconnected and refer to random pickings from your journal. We prefer the non-linear approach, which we find charming.

– But *pardon* you? That seems misplaced.

Ah. Right. We understand. It is only a manner of speaking. We shall be more careful.

Now Atta, we found much to like about you, and therefore we were a little surprised by the people round about you, Atta. A careful reading of your journal suggests that they were a wicked bunch for sure, but we wondered how did you manage to be hitched up with them in the first place? It was not your doing, surely. It did seem better at first, when you had friends, but then they drifted off, or was it you who weighed anchor? Then came the other people. Paraphrasing from different parts of your journal, we find indications that there was evil in their smiles. Their wickedness grew and grew, they struck you when you were down, they hit you when you were most vulnerable. They strove to shame you, having found your weaknesses. They said, "Shame on you Atta, you fixed it and it broke again, just after one trial." "You, Atta," they said, "you promised to stop drinking in January, it's past Easter now and you still drink at night, even at Lent you did not relent, oh Atta. Your own liver and you did not spare it." But Atta, you must have known that this is the way of the world, we all suffer at the hands of mockers, except that at a point you felt that all you had were those people – the ones who sought to do you in. Therefore, we conclude that you were paranoid. Do you agree?

– No.

But lonely, certainly.

– Obviously. Though I suspect that you have no idea how lonely one really is in life. How lonely. How far away love is. How dispossessed, each in his skull, how removed.

We have an idea of all that, Atta, at least from your journal. But now, in your current state, are you lonely?

– Emotion is currently invalid.

So we cannot annoy you?

– How could you?

We ask you.

– You may well ask.

We'll take that to be a no. In any case, we do not intend to annoy you, we only intend to interrogate your perspectives for this most important research. Now, there is a primary reason for this interview, which we can encapsulate in a single question. What is it like, to die? If you answered it now, and fully, half our work would be done.

– You will find out in time. It comes to one and all. A little patience, is all it takes.

Yes, but before it comes to us we would like to hear from you, so we can better prepare for the event.

– It is impossible to prepare for this event.

Very well, Atta. We shall move on. Are you sad that you are dead?

– No.

Happy?

– No.

Are you ambivalent, or is it that you are somehow unable to answer these questions?

– Some questions are inadmissible in the protocol, and therefore can only receive such replies.

So answering "yes" to the preceding couple would have been the same thing from your perspective?

– Yes.

That is a rather interesting situation, eh? Both yes and no being correct answers?

– Strange, maybe, when your rules of logic are limited.

Indeed, Atta. Human limitation, eh? There may be something beyond yes, no, and maybe so?

– And why not? Look at pi in relation to the rest.

Yes — we are looking at it, Atta, and will do so even more intently after this conversation.

Now Atta, we want to hear your thoughts on the summary of life, we want you to distil the very essence of life, to the extent of your powers. You, Atta, expired after a relatively sad existence of middling length, now in a place that cannot be discovered, perhaps doing things that cannot be described, or having things done to you that cannot be mentioned, Atta, were we to ask for the sum of it all, what would you say?

– The final adjuration of Solomon is apt.

— Atta, let us move on to your career as a musician, which you truncated a few years before your departure from this life. Your career peaked, as it were, during the five and a half years you were with the rock band; but whoever heard of Ghanaian rock, Atta? Why did you and your friends attempt such a thing, were you not afraid of Ghanaians? Lord knows, even angels would baulk at testing this society.

– We were young and did not know what we were doing.

A fitting reply, Atta, we have no quarrel with that. We have also spoken to Kongi, your songwriter and lead singer. You recall your signature anthem, the song about wanting to fall through the universe and drift across the constellations, about us all being stardust?

– Yes.

Poignant, eh?

– Yes.

Do you recall the night the band performed that song before a booing crowd which thought your music too intellectual?

– Yes.

We read the newspaper article about that concert, you were the closing act. Were you disappointed by their reaction? Your journal just has a single word about that night: "Lonely."

– Yes.

You felt you couldn't connect?

– Yes.

What do you think about that event now? Should you have bothered about that?

– Yes.

Do you care to explain why?

– I do not care.

Very well. A day later your band got its big break. In your journal the observation of this rather important event is rather sedate. You did not want to celebrate?

– No.

This is from the entry: "Good for us that at least one man sees what we are really saying. Sees our yearning to break out of the mould. Our attempt to defeat the gravity that binds the mind." Yet did you not know, Atta, that even for physical escape from the earth one needs eleven kilometres per second, how much more for spiritual escape? What would it require for such, and while alive did you try? Did you fail? Atta, now beyond the point of death, did you make it into the cosmos? Ever?

– You ask me again a question outside the protocol.

Such things are the focus of our investigation. But let us proceed. We have seen the video of your concert at the Children's Park, one of your last, and people who were there on that day said that – on the conga – you played as one possessed, you struck the djembe like one deranged; Atta, were you high? Like the other members of the band, were you smoking ganja? We find no reference to drugs in your journal, and yet it was said that you all smoked, claiming that it made the notes come to life, that Mojaka on the bass could not strum unless he popo... Were you also like that Atta?

– The journal speaks for itself.

And not for you?

– I wrote the journal.

So it speaks for you. Well – don't get the wrong impression, we are not judgemental. We rather liked the video. We like your music too. It is – different. But returning to the question. Were you on drugs, or were you – we use this word advisedly – possessed?

– You do not use the word advisedly enough.

And that is all you have to say?

– Yes.

We spoke to Kingsley, who we found alive and well in Stuttgart, and he told us about a most intriguing experiment you carried out. He thinks that you were never the same after that. Now Atta, and let us know the full facts if you please, your journal is mostly silent on this matter. Kingsley says you asked the band to 'make the soundscape, to immerse into the purest sound,' and when they declined you went ahead and did it all alone. You played music for days in a specially darkened room and would not come out, and you listened to a single tuning fork vibrating at A, at 432 Hz in fact.

– It was of no consequence.

Then what happened? What happened? In your journal you wrote "It happened." Only that one entry after a fortnight, only two words, after this great experiment. What happened?

– Why don't you try it yourself?

Why don't you tell us?

– The room was not dark, it was black. At the end I lightened it slowly, over many hours, to preserve my eyes. The presence in the room that I had felt after my first few days in the blackness and which had become increasingly oppressive in the final days was revealed to be a man standing in the corner.

There is no record of this in the journal. Who was this man? Was he corporeal?

– I have no idea. I fled. For all I know he is still there.

He is not there. We have been to that location, and all we found was mostly lizard shit. And dead roaches. Gathering dust is an understatement, the room was thick with it. But the place was generally undisturbed, recognisable for the room it was. Indeed, the tuning fork was still there, as was the turntable, and Led Zeppelin's stupid album was still under the needle.

– Oh well.

And even from later experience, and having gone through the transition, you still have no idea who this presence was?

– I could guess.

Do.

– No.

Atta, you toy with us, these are the important bits of data we seek for our research. We need to know.

– But you do not need to know, you do not need to know anything, even what you want to know is unnecessary.

Tell us about your divorce from music. It was incredible, and we did not quite understand it, given that music was almost god to you. Here in your journal it says, "It is over, the band will disperse. Tonight, the quarrel was bitter indeed. Fuck you! Mojaka shouted and smashed his guitar into the drum set. Mojaka loves his guitar. Kusi was trembling with rage. Every one was upset. I said goodbye and left. The sun was setting, and the sky was red." And we find recorded in your journal a few hours later, the words in a shaky scrawl, "...and so it is over between us as well, my true love." That must have been a terrible time Atta, a brutal transition, the day you said goodbye to music, and we wonder how could you have accepted such a decision when clearly music was the medium through which you sought removal from the terrestrial sphere? Were you then condemning yourself to be earthbound stardust?

– And you suppose that I could condemn myself?

A manner of speaking, Atta. What was the point then, of denying yourself the joy of making music? Was it even possible, really?

– More things are possible than you could ever imagine.

Granted, but what was the point?

– There was no point. It was time.

Did you realise that then, or after you died?

– You must understand that there is no difference.

No difference? How do you mean?

– I have said what I mean.

We shall move on, Atta. Here is something else, from Volume 9, January to May. "Front facing the storm I refuse to be cowed." Page 124, the last entry, on May 5. You wrote, "The darkness is settling in the land, and I, Atta, where can I be found?" We are curious about these words, Atta, what was this darkness? Did you have a premonition? Did you speak in metaphor?

– The darkness still descends, it is always descending, those before me saw darkness descending and yet I thought it was light, their darkness.

Wait. You mean all the way back, at the beginning, there was so much more light? And at the end, there will be darkness? Total darkness, perhaps? Is that what you have just said?

– What I have said, I have said.

Atta, you toy with us.

– As you wish.

Not so.

– Not so.

Atta, you know that people said things about you. Some more true than others. You worried about what people thought about you, but why did it matter so much? You wrote about the impenetrable barrier of the cranium, and we agree with you, yet from where you have gone to sit, was it important at all, this worry about what other people thought about you?

– Yes.

Very well, Atta. Now tell us how it was, when you dreamed that you had died. The journal entry was terse. "The worst fucking thing ever. I dreamed I had died."

– It is impossible to describe this to you.

We persist nevertheless. Do indulge us.

– I was falling. Into darkness so black it transcends imagination. And I thought, I have so much to left to do, and everything is so out of reach. It was clear that the separation was without bound. Yet I could recall everything about myself. I thought about the plans I had made for the days ahead. Then I felt a great terror, and wrenched out of the dream, and lay panting in bed. And night after night after that I could not sleep, out of fear. It was unpleasant and beyond description.

Thank you for that, Atta. It is a very important bit of information. Now this was many years before the fact of your passing away. When you actually died, was it anything like that?

– Yes, but there was more.

Do tell.

– No.

Atta, when we put together your entire story, we were saddened by the depth of your loneliness – how harsh! How bitter your life was! Do you know you were committed to the other side attended only by a constable a little under the influence, 'a tippler out of respect for the unknown deceased' he said, a digger, and a priest pressed upon to commit you, the dead stranger? A priest only because of the rosary about your neck, a priest sympathetic after vespers, and ashes to ashes, Atta, in the falling rain, in that churchyard far away from home.

– Your speech is mellifluous.

Indeed. The panel has applauded.

– But they treated me with respect, those three. Buried me as if they were burying themselves. I met them too late. Had I met them while alive, the prospects might have been interesting.

We discovered from our investigation, that that morning, while the rain clouds hung heavy and the light drizzle wet everything, the constable went knocking at the door of the rectory. "It is a terrible thing, Father. A man has died, and must now be buried." The priest replied, "The day is taken up with meetings and visitations, if you do not mind, let us perform the operation in the afternoon."

– How quaint.

Yet you were no angel, Atta. Perhaps the bile, the build-up of a lifetime of bitterness made you... offensive? Was there a hidden hatred in you, Atta?

– This is victim baiting.

Perhaps, all your complaints about other people could be linked to your character? In a sinuous linking of cause and effect? Your beastliness often touched the phenomenal. Surely, you recall Anna, and how you treated Anna the first time that you met her? The woman your mother brought to you? Anna was a good girl, Atta. Yet you cast about the room with a wild look in your eye, shouting, Is this the promised cunt? Atta, screaming at your mother after meeting the arranged bride. And you threw them out.

– I knew Anna beforehand, in ways my mother did not imagine.

Did not imagine? Could not imagine, your mother, with all her years, Atta? We have interviewed your mother, and we found her loving, patient, and wise.

– Your thoroughness must be admired.

Your behaviour that evening was shabby, to say the least. Anna wept.

– So did I.

Why do you do not ask about your mother, or Anna?

– There is no need to.

Would you like to see them?

– There is no need to.

Very well, Atta. Let us return to Anna. We have spoken to her. She is pretty, even now. She is smart and thoughtful. We found out, that even at the time she came to you she was not spoilt by the ways of the world. And she came of her own free will, to be trothed.

– I knew Anna, not as she was but as she would be. And my outburst was justified.

Oh Atta, now you intrigue us. You mean to say that you saw the future?

– What I have said, I have said.

You toy with us, Atta.

– Not so.

How about revenge, Atta? Is there any one upon whom you would like to exact a just revenge? Do you wish to avenge yourself? You were treated abominably by some people, Atta. Kpesese for example, bore false witness against you in order to save his job. He still lives, and says he is quite happy. We have spoken to him in his mansion up in the Aburi mountains overlooking the Accra plains. The view from there is phenomenal. Or perhaps the view is better from where you are? You see, we have no idea about these things. In any case, returning to Kpesese, he retired early, and lives in his mansion with his family. Now how about revenge, Atta; do you seek it? Or some form of justice, at least, Atta? The salve of retribution, maybe?

– I want none of it, this thing you suggest. And do not speak to me about justice, because it is clear you do not understand it, and you are incapable of understanding it.

Why can't we understand justice?

– Perhaps you overestimate your ability to appreciate certain concepts.

So you have no regrets?

– Regret? That is of no consequence.

Why?

– What use is it? What will it achieve, regret?

Very well, Atta. To other matters now. Sex has always been a delicate matter and so we rightly tread this ground lightly. It would appear that you had sex four times in your life – we ask this question just for statistical purposes, we hold no opinions on this matter. Is this datum correct? You do not speak? Atta? Very well, we proceed. You see, there is a small element of doubt because even though each encounter is recorded in the journal – we added them up and got four – it is possible that on such an issue a journal record might just be inaccurate. Is it accurate? Atta? Very well then. We found something rather curious in your journal, Atta. It makes us suspect that you knew before you died that you were going to die, that something momentous was going to happen to you. This is also because your last journal entry was precisely one month before you died. On May 3, two days before your last entry, we find what is effectively a summing up of your life – some aspects of it at least. We find, for example, "No.

of countries visited – 4. No. of times attended church (age 7 upwards) – 1,144. Never driven a car. No. of times Bible read – 5. No. of books read – 3,030. Owned: 1 Technics turntable, Grundig amplifier and speaker set. 1 Yamaha DX-7 keyboard. 2 djembe. No. of friends – 0. No. of enemies – 0." It goes on and on, covers one and a half pages, all told. But right at the end we find, "Sax – 4 times. (But some have 0)." There was a little confusion amongst we the investigators at this point. Four times on the saxophone? But you did not play wind. This confusion was somewhat cleared up by the illustration on the next page. There are quite a few illustrations in your journal, they are quite well done we must say. This particular illustration was of a well-endowed female. If the illustration represents your taste you ought to be congratulated. In itself the drawing suggested little, but underneath it, in florid writing, was the exclamation, "nyash!" This was enough to settle the matter – we came to collective agreement that "sax = sex" in this instance. The question is, and we ask only to satisfy certain statistical considerations, did you really have sax four times in your life? if so, were there any reasons for this? Also, from your new perspective as a dead man, Atta, what is the importance of sax in life?

Atta?

– My Bible was the King James version, I had just one copy. Always started with the Gospels, followed by the Revelation, and then the Epistles. After that the Old Testament, Proverbs, and I saved the Psalms for last. I read it five times over.

Now Atta, we did say at the beginning that we would not follow a line of enquiry concerning sax, but having started we feel we must do more than scratch at the surface, there does seem to be a rich node to be mined here, some important information can be received that the living will surely benefit from. The record shows that there were two women, and sax was achieved, once with one and thrice with the other. "Achieved" is your own word, Atta. Now – Ahem. Well, to read from the journal – do we embarrass you, Atta? Surely, you must know that is not our intention. We have only the greatest respect for you, and we really appreciate your spending time with us, taking our questions. Where you are, is it in the afternoon as it is here? Or it is morning perhaps? We suspect that time would be meaningless for you at the other side, but what do we know, Atta, what do we know? Right. You prefer that we proceed? What does your silence mean? Very well. We move on, the woman in this case is Joanna. You wrote, "Congress proceeded with eyes shut." Whose eyes were shut? Yours? If yes, why so? Even the little aspects are of interest to us, much can be learnt from an examination of the microscopic.

We are a little bothered by your silence, Atta. You have not spoken in a while. Have we offended you? But you indicated you were beyond offence. Are we wasting your time? But you suggested that that was impossible. You do not like us? But we were developing such great rapport! We plead with you Atta, because we cannot threaten you, nor can we compel you, we have not the tools. Even so, we prefer the friendly approach, much is to be said for the soft touch.

But Atta, you must speak, answer the questions! Atta, you are spoiling the research! You must answer our questions. This is important, do you not see? How the answers will change everything? All at once? Don't you see that this going on around in circles, has been of little use? And now your silence threatens to incapacitate the entire effort. We might as well just publish your journal, Atta. Talk to us. We are alive, we need help. Won't you help us to understand? How it all is? How it all ends, at least? Please? Shall we sing our questions? Shall we bring your old friends here? Some of them are still alive. Atta!

THE WAITING

I AM WAITING for my name to be called. This is the current situation. Why am I sure of it? First, the nature of the room in which I am suggests that I must be waiting, for my name to be called out, by someone, or by some machine, or by some other entity, example, God, Angel, Demon, Satan, my grandfather sadly gathered unto God, and so on... and when my name is called as described I shall proceed to the next stage of the matter, in the manner of a progression, linear, non-linear, random, logical, and so on...

Second, I am sure that I am waiting to be called because this is what makes the most sense to me, in any case this room resembles one in which persons sit and wait to be called, so that they can participate in the next matters, as previously mentioned. Like a hospital or perhaps the condemned cells in a prison: in the final hours before the execution, one imagines that the prisoner, about to be killed at the pleasure of the state, would wait also in such a manner as I am waiting now, perhaps after a final meal delivered for the sake of humanity, one wonders why they don't just send someone sneaking in at night with a dagger, the state does worse things, who the hell do they wish to deceive with their hypocrisy?

But to return to the matter at hand, which is that this room is a waiting room, designed for me alone, no one else can use it – designed by whom? God, perhaps? He is the usual suspect in such matters but I reckon the most immediate architect of this room is myself, no, this requires further explanation because starting off on the right foundation yields much benefit later, for example there will arise no need to unlearn faulty axioms. The premises of the argument must therefore be sound, all things must be properly defined and so on, this is my strong belief, the fact of the matter is that I do not know who designed this room, but I seem to be able to occupy it at will. The design and construction of the room is rather unique, there is much that is curious about it: it is obviously not of physical construct, but of the fact that it is real there is no doubt, since I can see it, and I am in it. The room is so damn clean I feel like an impurity, I cannot remark hotness or coldness so I am sure that the temperature is just right, to a fraction of a degree perhaps, the walls are stark white now but I can change the colour at will, but that is all I can do, I am, as it were, rooted – no, bound is a better word, trapped by an intense force between my buttocks and the seat is another description, in any case I am unable to remove myself from the cushion on which I am seated. Pardon me, it may not be a cushion at all because it is hard and yields little to the pressure of my buttocks, it may in fact be a box, made of metal or wood or marble, just like the walls of the room, just like the door, just like the ceiling. The room itself is a cuboid, I am seated at one end of it, and at the far end there is a faint trace in the white of the wall, a rectangular trace, flush with the wall, which must be the door through which my name will be called, and most likely through which I will proceed to participate in the subsequent matters.

I must have come here by myself. Did I will it, or was I compelled? Could I ever tell, and would it even matter, is it not better to instead consider the grave matter of what happens next, the indeterminable near future, the externals of which are truly out of my control? But I have gained mastery of my thoughts, and so I create, and so I live, and so I proceed... This room is a box, I am inside a box, but it is so spacious it cannot be a coffin, but were it a coffin would I still be thinking? Would I not instead be rotting, would I still know I was waiting, waiting for my name to be called? But it is not a coffin because I could not have died and been buried unawares, though that possibility can not be altogether rejected, because what is death like? No man has returned to report, so this could just be it. But let me not leave out the finer details. There is no visible source of lighting, yet the room is well lit, I can see everything, from stark white wall to stark white wall, but there is a sheen is there not? The walls seem to weep a soft whiteness, the walls, the ceiling, the floor, all white, stark white, weeping a glow, but damn it, it is sublime, just some Beethoven and it would be complete, yet why Beethoven? is there no music equivalently sublime? Perhaps there is, but certainly not the drums, not the atumpan and those thumping things, hollow bits of wood covered with dried animal skin, oh the ugliness of that would be so out of place in this place, would not match at all the sparkling cleanliness of this room, such heathen instruments belong to clearings in the forest with bare feet trampling in dust and smelly half-naked bodies glistening with sweat, and shrill voices screaming some lustful songs, short and repetitive and earthy songs, which brings me face to face with the fact that this place is certainly a far-flung outpost of the world, maybe it's the very edge of the spirit world, notorious for its non-existence, for being the eternal prick that man kicks against, and don't I like the sound of that, the eternal prick. It must have some significance.

Such disdain for your culture, the Priest says, you must be ashamed. I tell the Priest, Cognitive dissonance is a coping strategy for GhanaMan: why, take a look at yourself, a Priest of the church in Rome, you have cast away the religion of our people, and you complain when I disdain the drum? But there is one true God, the Priest declares, But not one true drum, I interject. The Priest replies, What I want to talk about is this cognitive dissonance thing that you have just raised. It is quite simple really, I reply, but no, the Priest insists on a full answer. It is a schizophrenia, I declare, We are fake each time we speak, and think: who owns the thought if the language is alien?

I have spoken of the Priest without proper introduction, but this little error is easily remedied, although it requires a further description of the current situation. Having entered into this place I conjure whom or what I please, and I move in this new space with ease: I socialise, I explore, and technically fun is possible but I have not yet realised such, nor bothered with such. I shall focus on important items and to help me do this, I present the Priest, of Jesuit persuasion no less, and the Air Vice Marshal, a Scot with an ancestry deeply involved in the colonial history of the west coast of Africa, soldiering and raping being counted amongst the valiant deeds of his forebears. Circumstance has made the Scot a naturalised African, and he is the military advisor to the head of state of some mango republic on the west coast, which position consisted of God-knows-what, because the Scot himself did not know what, he spent his time wandering about in the corridors and offices of the Ministry of Defence sleeping through meetings and drawing a fat salary, so it was worth his while, enough! The Priest, an honest chap, delighted in the things of the Lord, I loved to poke fun at him, swell fellow though, tall and lanky and quite handsome, enough! Sometimes we take a walk along the beach, and I would have removed all unwanted human beings as a matter of course, making it possible to stroll leisurely along the quiet expanse, and have a discussion, and partake in the well-aged Scotch provided by the Air Vice Marshal, who in addition would puff at a huge cigar, puff, at a huge cigar. Oh what landscapes have we not explored! Imagine a terrible expanse of snow and ice, stretching around, about, and we sat there the three of us, right in the middle! Or crammed into a toilet cubicle, again we three, listening to the occupant of the next grunting and farting – sometimes illumination comes in the weirdest places, enough!

We can go anywhere I want.

So it is possible that I am waiting for an angel to call my name and usher me into the presence of God. Or perhaps into the presence of Yesu Kristo, recently late of Nazareth, nailed to the cross by the murderous Romans through the scheming of Caiaphas and his gang, cheered on by hapless crowds of Jews who were seeking the Messiah but wouldn't let pass the little bit of gory entertainment, betrayed by Judas and denied by Peter, let down by Pilate, but, man, didn't he suffer, the Son of God for the sake of man? This is a mystery, said the Priest, observing the scone in his hand as if it were the bread before it was dipped into the wine and eaten, and I add, I hope he still does not suffer, the Redeemer, look at all these wicked people in the world who seem not to appreciate this great sacrifice.

Maybe it is Yesu who I am going to meet, and perhaps it is judgement next, boy, and then what? What? Perhaps I will see the entity over there, in the great hall where the judgement will be held, but why a hall, why not a large open space floating in the cosmos, with billions of stars sparkling all about, I prefer such a place to a hall no matter how grand, but what have I seen, who am but a man? yet I prefer such, I know I do, I know I do. I shall describe the picture I have in my mind of meeting God, not now, but later, later.

Let me get the matter of the entity out of the way, the mugu which has been responsible for much pain and suffering in my life and dare I say it crafted the path that leads me from one disaster to the other – except perhaps I am not so sure that it is this entity or that entity for surely there must be more than one mugu in an infinite universe, let us not limit the boundaries it may even be the case that there is an entity that is looking after me and is concerned about my welfare but that is all beside the fucking point what I am saying is that maybe I shall see the entity over there, at the place where there is the Judgement, when to each according to his deeds, to pain or to bliss, fire and brimstone or living water and streets of gold and haven't I had enough of this already? I say to the Priest and he replies, Well you have no idea, and I said no I mean it and the Priest says Well you haven't any idea how hard it is to pee in a hurry when you are in this cassock, especially when it is hot and you are sweating and the bladder is straining it takes much self control to restrain yourself from raising one end of the skirt and letting go, letting go, but what is this about an entity? Then I declare to the Priest, I believe in demon possession, and the Priest is quick to reply, Oh exorcism is practised in the church you can be freed. The Priest turns to the Air Vice Marshal, his wrinkled octogenarian self on vacation in Ghana. He was a well-known homosexual who was often content just to have his haunches stroked after which he would take a walk with his dog while puffing at his Cuban cigar, and so did life pass. The Priest says, He believes in demons but is not sure about God. Well, stranger things have been known, the Air Vice Marshal replies. I have wondered, I say to the pair who have drawn closer and are looking at me with amusement, would there be enough demons to go around, seeing as the world population is exploding, and the number of demons finite? What an absurd thought, the Priest says, Absurd indeed, the Air Vice Marshal echoes, but I insist in putting forward my thesis, which is that a demon can do an effective job of harassing a man and ruining his life by nudging just at the right time to cause destruction, spoiling just the smallest thing at the correct time to cause great misery, the canker-worm also comes to mind, something small that gnaws is also an associated thought. Consider as an example the case of a young man, let us call him Philemann, a broke young University graduate, unemployed for many years, a serial writer of application letters, he has sent four hundred and thirty-three letters and worn out five pairs of shoes trudging from office to office, sometimes he gets to meet the Managing Director, sometimes the Human Resource Manager, and sometimes he meets only the receptionist who makes faces at him, in any case Philemann is down on his luck and often hungry, Philemann one morning finds a letter in the mail from an Insurance Company, Dear Philemann, the letter says, In response to your application &c, I am pleased to offer you a place &c, I invite you to meet the interview panel &c, and on the appointed day Philemann dresses up in his best, superglue serves to hold the sole of his right shoe together because it is only for the afternoon, but the tro-tro breaks down on the way, and then he has to walk, and trot, and then the shoe gives up, so now the sole is halfway off and Philemann has to make sure that his right foot comes down on the flat and this makes his walking rather contorted, but he manages a fair pace anyway, and soon he is approaching the building on the second floor of which the interview panel is gathered, and one member of the panel looks out of the window and sees Philemann walking like a camel and he says Good Lord! Take a look at the man down there, and the entire panel crowds round the window and everyone collapses in wicked mirth, and only fifteen minutes later Philemann is seated before them, face shining with sweat. OK maybe not the greatest example but imagine Philemann does not get the job, or maybe he gets rained on and misses the interview, and so on, and he ends up accusing God for all the bad luck, well that is the work of the mugu, a demon who does not possess you and therefore cannot be exorcised but ruins you all the same. What an interesting thought, the Priest says, even if poorly articulated, Haw, it is a curious thought, the Air Vice Marshal agrees.

I am not dead of course. Have I said that already? Then I will say it again. I have retracted into the quiet spaces in my mind, and it does not matter what the actual state of things is out there, the important thing is that I am in control and can focus on the really really important things, obviously this is the sort of state that oriental gurus strive for, crossed legs and straggly beards and glazed eyes and you can tell they are just making believe with all the mumbojumbokumbohambo but seriously I am here and I don't care again what is happening outside my mind, happening to my body, perhaps I have had a stroke and I am a vegetable in the hospital and the nurses are masturbating my prick; who knows what health professionals get up to in the silent hours of the night, the security cameras notwithstanding? There we go. To detach from the body and enter into the true state of existence in the mind, that is the pinnacle. Yet despite these brave words I must still allow for the possibility that I am already dead, for the terrible thing about death is that it is eternal wakefulness and not eternal sleep, no more sleep at all, and perhaps all that one would have is this room to himself, but I am not dead! even though it must come soon enough, soon enough, let me not pre-empt the arrival of that singularity.

In this room I can make things up out of nothing. That much is clear by now. Let us consider the case of a thin old man, a bachelor even at his age, a professor it must be said, of previously imposing stature one must add, judging from his now straggly but once luxuriant beard, he having dedicated his whole adult life to the study of the topological applications of Banach's theorem, a clever man no doubt, whose knowledge the Examinations Council tapped for the setting of questions for the Additional Mathematics paper. Witness then this man, at his desk, inking the words Suppose, (PART A, Question 1, item i.,) that a bead is projected down a wire whose equation is $f(y) = cosh(y)$, with an initial speed u, and that it is subject to a force of friction directly proportional to its instantaneous velocity v, in the limit that v is less than one tenth of the terminal velocity of a small solid sphere in free fall, and to a force of friction proportional to the square of v, if v is greater than that terminal velocity, shew that..., and the professor of mathematics pauses and says, what am I doing, are these not 'A' level students, this is a small matter for them, but at this time my problem has to do with the fact that my cat has been missing for a day and a half, which has caused me great distress, but who knows one of the students might have a similar problem, perhaps even a related problem, or a connected problem, it is even possible that the student in question has killed and eaten my cat, in which case he must be punished, and therefore the difficulty of the question must be increased, so help him God. Let the equation be $f(y) = 2sinh(y)+cosh(y)$, all it does is to make the wire lorgor, in addition though shall we cause the wire to rotate slowly about the long axis with angular velocity ω, there, so the student who has eaten my cat will sweat profusely, regardless of what he has to shew.

Now let me proceed to generate a parable out of this. Observe the manner in which the professor's life comes to an end, it is most tragic indeed. He, a teetotaller all his life right to the bitter end, was done to death by drink, even if indirectly. And this is how the sad event occurred. Master Markus Danglais, a brilliant student it must be admitted, even at his age having masterful control over the calculus of variations and having single-handedly solved in his childhood the brachistochrone problem before he had even heard of it, now having successfully completed the 'A' level Additional Mathematics paper, and shewn, in different ways, that the bead in Part A, Question 1, item i., would become motionless after a short time, that in Part A, Question 1, item ii., the molecular dumbbell would be stuck in the potential energy well for all time, and demonstrated other things besides, decides to celebrate the ease with which he wrote the paper by having a meal of jankple with grilled joseph and draining a bottle of London Dry Gin with two other young men, after which they jump into a car, a Volkswagen Beetle it is, and drive it at great speed through the streets of Ho, and sad to say, knock down, run over, and kill the venerable professor as he crosses the road in front of the Post Office. I turn this case over to the Priest and the Air Vice Marshal, who are immediately excited by it, and consider it a good introduction to the topic of death, and the Priest says, Death is the one thing to ponder about, we must examine the nature of it, the meaning of it, the realisation of it, one must contemplate it but it is not enough, for God cannot be separated from it, also it is deceptive to think that science and philosophy are about anything else, for really these are the ultimate questions. I agree with the Priest, because even if I was capable of knowing everything I would want to find out really what is death? and could I die and resurrect? and if I did then would I actually have been dead? it is a matter to exercise every mind, and that is why I am here, shut off from all the pettiness of living, in this white box – well, it's a room in my mind I suppose, the clarity is intense and I can conjure again the Air Vice Marshal and the Priest, and where are we this time? it is in the late afternoon, the sun earlier scorching is now mild, we are seated at the edge of a crag and the Shai Hills rear up around and fall off below to the distant plains. Verdant grassland says the Priest, taking a sip of the Scotch kindly provided by the Air Vice Marshal, and as I expound on this important topic of death the Air Vice Marshal interjects, Well if you died you would not notice, really. Interesting point, the Priest says, but quite untrue, you will know very well that you have died, perhaps you will appreciate even more keenly your existence when you are faced with the reality of purgatory, and then Hell, or Heaven. Stop, I plead, It does not bear thinking about, do you know eternity, what it means? Timelessness! the Priest cries, that is how you must look at it. A stationary quantum state, the Air Vice Marshal says, and so physics proves true in the afterlife as well. What interests me though, says the Air Vice Marshal, is the anticipation of death. I used to wonder about this during the war, seeing all those young men thundering off to likely death in the Spitfires, and those other young men in the Messerschmitts. There is a wider philosophy in the matter, of being, at least. War brings such thoughts powerfully to the forefront, the Priest remarks, Ideology transits through musculature. Not all wars, the

Air Vice Marshal counters, some just fill you with disgust. For example, the recent civil war in my country, with rebels crushed by the greater firepower of the state, there was nothing philosophical to be gleaned at any level, at all. The poor devils, led by Commander-Messiah something or the other, a rag-tag bunch marching through the bush, attacking police posts with AK 47s and machetes. And the glorious army of the state noted the ethnicity of the rebels, and decided to use their air force to solve the problem. Their Air Force! All they had were a couple of MiGs, and oddly enough, the rebels had some ack-ack of indeterminate age and manufacture, more danger to the gunners than the aircraft, why fight a stupid war like that in any case? Well, so the MiGs went in with the cannon, strafed a few villages at will, and of course there were no rebels there, they just killed a bunch of villagers, it was – pass me the Scotch, will you – in the end it was just niggers fighting some meaningless war. I protest! the Priest cries, Did you just say nigger? It was only the American in me that said so, the Air Vice Marshal replies, it was the redneck in me that said so. And what would the Boer in you have said? the Priest says sarcastically, and the sparkle in the Air Vice Marshal's eye is not due to drink.

The Priest strokes his bushy black beard grown after the fashion of Kristo for surely the son of man sported a growth, for how would he have shaved in the absence of Gillette True Blue? Perhaps in the matter of comparing beards, Kristo might not be a proper metric since I have not seen him before, not even a photograph certified to be the true likeness of Yeshua bar Yehoseph, never mind that weird bit of calico from Turin who knows what that thing really is, but Marx! Yes! The writer of the Communisto Manifest, he sported a bushy beard, did not all those communists from Russia, they looked so sexy, ah! Lenin, Trotsky, all them goddam dems, in varying lushness, the beard! That was the trick, though Stalin preferred a moustache, but that must have been due to the influence of his Teutonic opposite. Those reliefs from Mesopotamia, showing the Nebuchadnezzans with flaring beard, yes, in that manner is the beard of the Priest, and now that this matter has been cleared up, the Priest strokes his beard. And it is the subject of Death, says the Priest, that forces upon man the acceptance of God. The Air Vice Marshal disagrees. Death, he argues, is real enough, we see it often enough, God on the other hand, but the Priest allows none of that, The existence of God cannot be denied, he declares, even the collective consciousness of man admits this. The Air Vice Marshal replies with smoke emanating from his cigar, Since it has so far been impossible to show as fact the existence of God, I am free to assume that the reason for his persistence in the human psyche is that an entity not alive cannot be dead, and must therefore persist. I pray thee but that is bullshite right there, the Priest is getting angry, The question of the death of God does not arise, I say, applying calmative. The Priest protests, his tone severe: let the Air Vice Marshal beware of false logic! Blast that, the Air Vice Marshal returns, we might as well worship Satan for what the whole thing is worth, Such blasphemy, says the Priest, Do you not feel hell-fire on your arse already? Now you mention it I realise me balls be singed, the Air Vice Marshal replies, the fiery blast must have been misdirected, an infernal error to be sure.

This thing is listing where I would it rather not, listing towards God, and OH WERE I ABLE TO PUT HIM OUT OF MY MIND but it is impossible, I say, and my compatriots seem amused. Teeheehee the hound of God, the Priest declares, you shall never be free until you give in, Only a broken Will can enter the Kingdom of God. I take a different view, the Air Vice Marshal says, you suffer a crisis imposed by the medieval thinking of the old countries, your torment is entirely European in origin – I sympathise, but if you pray to an alien God in a foreign language why do you despair when he does not reply?

I now approach another aspect of this matter. What if my name is called, and I finally am able to rise, pass through the door, and then it is none other but God at the other side? floating perhaps on a sparkling cloud and coils of electricity twirling about, also the incense must not be forgotten, and then... and then, he will speak to me! Lord God! At last, I shall cry – *Abba*! I shall want to grab his feet and weep – but of course I can't – but maybe I can! After I have wept, overwhelmed, we shall have a conversation, which is what I have always wanted to do, the impossibility of this notwithstanding, for Jobean pretensions aside, what does a man talk to the Creator of the Universe about? Infinities cannot be comprehended. Observe the tail of cosmic dust extending a hundred million light years, slowly spiralling around the billion solar mass black hole in the middle of that dwarf galaxy directly above the galactic plane of the Milky Way, God says, I shall send my trusted hound to fetch a small cluster of neutrinos for my amusement. Then perhaps dumbstruck I would have nothing to say to the Creator, even though I really would like to ask, Is it really important which way the kite flies? and then perhaps He will reply and say No, son, so long as it goes around the burning market, and then I would ask what about if there is no burning market, or if the kite passes the other way, and perhaps He would smile and say, What if there is no kite, or no market? God, smiling, what a wonderful thing to behold.

Of people there are currently seven billions on the planet, if each person were to hold a conversation with God, perhaps for ten minutes, why that already is seventy billion minutes, and how many hours is that? We proceed with the long division. Seven divided by six is one remainder one to which we add a zero, six into ten is one remainder four, to which we add a zero, six into forty is six remainder four, yes, we see where we are now. So in hours we have one point one six six six and so on billion hours, and how many days is that? But I decline to do this arithmetic; where is Master Markus Danglais when he is needed?

Of course, this is only my thinking. For all I know it must be the easiest thing for God to speak in 3,412-letter words made of consonants perhaps and maybe even the language will not be English but instead Mandarin or Arabic in which case would God not be Allah but it is not Allah I speak about it is God, the same of whom I have been told since childhood, and who knows me quite well and I dare say is sometimes amused by my antics and my worries and he might be thinking in 5,000-letter words WHY IS THIS MAN SO CONCERNED ABOUT LITTLE THINGS?

Let me now move on to meet Yesu, who indeed is seated at the right-hand side of God, and since I am facing God Yesu appears to my left, Kristo seems altogether less terrible than his father, even though there is much to inspire awe, I mean to begin with he is shrouded in light, it seems to stream from every part of his body, and his features are so sharp, and his eyes, when he fixed them on me, cut to the bone. Unlike God Kristo is not smiling, but he is not frowning either he has this expressionless face, and it is hard to imagine what he is thinking but would that not be impossible? in any case, one cannot read thoughts from the face, furthermore Kristo is not a human being, or at least has not been for centuries, and for all we know has no further interest in repeating the experience. I kneel, O yes, at the mention of the name every knee shall bow etc., but it is the thing to do even though the name has not been mentioned, the majesty impels, O, Kristo, I say, so it is in order now to kneel, O Kristo, O Kristo, and Kristo says not a word.

In any case, why do I think that it is some ecclesiastical appointment for which I am about to be called instead of an infernal appointment? Well, that possibility must be considered. Let us make the setting right. If it were an infernal appointment, superintended perhaps by the devil himself, Satan no less, the decor would be different. Instead of the stark white of the walls and the ceiling, the creamy white of the floor and the thin shadow of the edges of the door in the

far wall, there is darkness and blackness. Black walls, black
floor, and the door delineated by a glowing blood-red line.
The scarlet glow illuminates the room with a rather macabre
hue, yet it is nice, a warm scarlet effervescence projecting into
the black black room, and when I hold up my hands I see the
fingers outlined in red, and oh I must admit it is rather sexy.
But now I am waiting for my name to be called, this time for
an appointment with the devil, and doesn't this thrill? it does
but it is in a different way than if it was God, for example I
expect that my name, when called, would boom and reverb
hollowly, and would be a little off-tone, like when a guitarist
is trying to tune his guitar and has not yet hit the correct
note so that the B flat sounds like bullshit. How shall Satan
be now, obviously Miltonian, no just somewhat Miltonian,
he is suave in a sharp black three piece suit, the infernal
version of a Pierre Cardin, obviously the population of Hell
must be put to work, his yellow eyes are tired, tired, and the
devil lights another cigarette. His hands are shaking. There
is a note of desperation in his voice. You do not know how
it is, says Satan, there is no way out. Then why did you call
me? I ask. Satan, pausing pacing, a hoary eyebrow rising,
I did? Did I? One wonders. Perhaps, an aural illusion. Oh
I am weary, he says. I cannot feel sorry for you, I say. No,
of course not, the devil agrees, Do you have answers? I ask,
Some, he replies. Will you indulge? I ask, Go ahead, he says,
taking a long draw at the cigarette, it is a Camel. I thought
they had stopped making them, I say, and the devil replies,
I am Satan after all, procuring a Camel is a small matter
for me. His cheeks glow with pride, scarlet lighting up the
ebony features. Why are human beings like that? I ask. Now
I remember! Satan cries, this is why I called you, I wanted to
ask you, why are black men like that? Like what? I retort, I
am a black man myself, perhaps you will rephrase, ask why
are people like that, Satan seems not to hear me, he goes on,
Consider, Satan says, the case of the venerable professor,
doubtless you know who I am talking about. Indeed I do, I
reply. A genius, Satan says wistfully, He is roasting in the

genius corner of Hell as we speak. You know why he was where he was when the VW Beetle under the control of Master Markus Danglais ran into him? Markus was at the wheel? I ask. Sadly, Satan replies, a place is now reserved for him in the genius corner as well. But the professor was on his way from an administrator's office. And for what reason had the professor gone to the administrator's office? Why, on account of his pension. It was the ninth time that month that the professor had been there. Unfortunately, said the administrator, your cheque is not ready. But you said the same thing last week, cried the professor, beside himself. The computer, the administrator said, had a problem. Impossible, the professor said, you are giving me excuses. Look at your nice shoe, said the administrator, and you bought it for you alone to wear. The cheque, the professor said, I want my cheque, it is my money, I worked for it, why are you doing this? I want to help you, said the administrator, licking his lips, the typist must have entered the wrong figure, you see, the computer has been programmed in such a way, entering the wrong figure, well, causes... The professor slammed his fist on the table. You importunate young man, he said to the administrator, a forty-five year old man, who at that very moment had in his drawer the cheque for the professor. The question, the devil asks, is why was the administrator behaving in such a base manner? I observe such things with surprise. I, amazed, ask, You, Satan, are surprised at such behaviour? I am, he says, lighting another Camel, they say I am evil, but I have style. Such worthless lying and other thievery, why, I have nothing to do with it. Who is to blame then? I ask, God? Of course not, Satan says, no one but man himself.

Very Good. Proceeding to other matters, I bring up for discussion with the Priest and the Air Vice Marshal, a small matter of historical note, concerning the time that I had constructed a register to keep track of insecticide, in this manner:

Mosquito Killing Register	
Day	Number of Mosquitoes Killed
Tuesday	5
Wednesday	8
Thursday	11
Friday	10
Saturday	12
Sunday	20

One would assume that my skill at destroying the bloody insects had grown by the sixth day, not to mention what would have happened on the seventh, had that not been my day of rest, it would seem that I had become more adroit at dispatching them, the fucking bloodsuckers. Such an assumption would not be entirely wrong but not entirely right either, because the fact of the matter was that on Saturday my father installed a fluorescent lamp in the room, and the brilliant white light made it easier to track the mosquitoes and squash them. Oh the delights of diving across the room and smacking them! Killing them! Revenge! Exacted! Turning to the Priest I say, You know the mosquito, and he replies, Indeed I do. Savage insect don't you think? I ask. Oh, yes I admit, but don't go there I know you're leading to ask why did God, yet you know that the world was cursed because of Adam, the Priest says. And Eve, the Air Vice Marshal interjects, worthless progenitors both. I tell the Priest, a mosquito bite while aware is devastating, not least to pride, oft times you slap at and miss, and insult is added to injury when you spot the little black spot dart off. Not to mention the ghastly malaria. My problem, I do not allow the Priest reprieve, is that mosquitoes bite children, does God know this? New born babes are not spared, their soft skin desecrated by the bite of so ugly a thing. Intriguing, the Air Vice Marshal comments, what do you say, Priest? Original sin means children are as guilty, the Priest whispers, and the

Air Vice Marshal says, I thought you would emphasise to our sceptical friend here, that God is not a mosquito, and cannot be held responsible. God rest the soul of Hideyo Noguchi, I begin, and all other researchers, fighting this insect. 'Twas the Aedes Egyptii knocked him off, the Air Vice Marshal adds, Not the Anopheles? the Priest asks, Certainly not the Culex, I snort, the man may have perished from other fevers, the Priest says, that would be more like it. How far is Japan from Ghana? the Air Vice Marshal asks. As the crow flies? the Priest asks. As the man walks. Or as the ship sails. What pushed him? Enquiry! Same as leads many to hell, but no one benefits from that – the Air Vice Marshal adds, Is there yellow fever in Japan? That is not the point, the Priest grumbles, You underestimate the potency of local medicine. My point, says the Air Vice Marshal, is why was a Japanese and not an African studying yellow fever to begin with. The disease is not endemic to, the Priest interjects, the virus is also to be found in the foetid swamps of South East Asia. Nevertheless, the Air Vice Marshal begins – I maintain, the Priest cuts in, there were local herbalists, and there was a remedy. Where is it? the Air Vice Marshal asks, Where is this remedy? A silence befalls. I erase this silence. The Air Vice Marshal shall speak now. The last words of Noguchi, the Air Vice Marshal says, were 'I do not understand.' And the last words of Goethe, I put in, were 'Light, more light.' And the last words of Christ, the Priest cries, were, 'My God, my God, why hast thou forsaken me?' And what did God say in reply, the Air Vice Marshal asks. It was not recorded, the Priest replies. But, I say to the Priest, Christ said other things in that darkest hour, did he not? I recall He said it was finished. It is in your Bible, the Priest says, John 19.30. What if he doesn't have a Bible? the Air Vice Marshal asks. But I have one, I say, complete with the Apocrypha, Bel and the Dragon is especially exciting.

Now I return to expand on the parable of the professor's last days, because he was done ill by others in addition to the accountant's execrable conduct. Before he met his end at the hands of Markus Danglais, the professor felt the walls already closing in, it was just a matter of time he knew, in the first place his friends had abandoned him, were they friends to begin with, and people he trusted had stabbed him in the back, a tired but tried and true metaphor, now witness Mr Q, in conversation with the professor in his office, Well my friend, said Mr Q, I trust everything goes well. So so, said the professor, but unbeknownst to him Mr Q had been spreading the most atrocious rumours, Mr Q had whispered to others, the professor is dying, his kidney you know, not to mention his pancreas, a cancer in his prostrate as well, in any case his character is appalling, he does young women in exchange for exam questions. I have good news for you, Mr Q told the professor. What is this? I exclaim to the Air Vice Marshal and Priest, this story is no good. I truncate the telling. Fuck Mr Q and his ilk, on behalf of the professor of course, What do you think? I ask my compatriots, Fuck him, says the Air Vice Marshal, I concur, says the Priest. Mr Q is now fucked in toto. So when the VW bore down on the Professor with a Hitlerian thu-thu-thu thu-thu, he was not entirely surprised, though he was really sad that it had to end this way. The final thoughts of the professor were rather drab and not at all illuminating. The professor thought, A road in Ghana can be crossed, perpendicular to the flow, in seven steps. Seven steps, yet here comes a Beetle, Ah shite!

Now is the time to kill my compatriots. The Air Vice Marshal first, that will be more dramatic. Then the Priest, for he must also die, him walking about with such confidence and committing others to the grave and such, yes, he shall also expire, by my powers, this is my world, my creation, and I do not will that he lives on. Air Vice Marshal. Stricken with one of the many diseases that afflict the old, pneumonia or bronchitis or some kidney distress or some liver problem not to mention arrhythmic beating of the heart as a precursor to an attack, or Alzheimer's, or a stroke, no no no I require that he is reasonably lucid to the bitter end, in any case, his physician, an acerbic Ghanaian trained in Aberdeen where he gained a hearty disrespect for the attitude of the white man towards other races, said to himself, Fucke this olde man, why must I waste resources on him, and therefore consigned the Air Vice Marshal to death in the posh private ward in a hospital in Accra, it was to this location that the Priest hurried to deliver the last rites, the Air Vice Marshal being a famously lapsed Catholic who had also spent his late twenties in the Church of England before realising he had a limited time to fuck and defenestrating religion altogether to make up for lost time etc., the Air Vice Marshal lay propped up against the pillows staring at the green wall opposite, and the doctor had been kind enough to provide a mild opiate and a saline drip. My God, said the Air Vice Marshal, it is here at last. The Priest held his hand, it was pale and grey and moist with sweat and almost lifeless, There may not be much time, said the Priest, do you believe in Christ? But I cannot see him no matter how hard I try, said the Air Vice Marshal, You were baptised and confirmed in the Church, said the Priest, Hell is not for such as you, Yes, said the Air Vice Marshal weakly, I was an altar boy, a mass server, God bless Father MacCarthy... his voice drifted off, and the Priest said, an urgent note creeping into his voice, you must confess if you can, else I shall proceed, there was a silence, the Air Vice Marshal had closed his eyes, the Priest wondered was he slipping already and he picked up the Holy Oil, but then the Air Vice Marshal's voice reached out dreamily, I believe in God. I believe in Jesus Christ and the Holy Spirit and the Immaculate Conception. And I am heartily sorry for all the sins I have committed, and the wrongs I have done... Enough! the Priest whispered fiercely and asked, Do you repent? And the Air Vice Marshal whispered, tears flowing from underneath his shut eyelids, Yes, and the Priest raised the oil and said, a glow of triumph in his eye, I absolve you in the name of the Father, and of the Son, and of the Holy Ghost. Needless to say the Air Vice Marshal expired soon after, to the grim delight of the Ghanaian doctor who thought, another fucker to his grave. Now to the Priest. He lived in a neighbourhood of Accra where the owner of a Gas Filling

Station had broken the law and bribed his way into putting up an liquefied petroleum gas dispensing plant just a street away from where the Priest lived. There were four 45,000 litre tanks of gas under high pressure there, and one of the tanks had sprung a leak, a welded joint was failing, for which it is entirely possible to blame entropy. And for some reason related to the fact of the inconceivable stochastic event that nevertheless occurs on account of very very large numbers, for example, the evolution of man, a small spark jumped across the leak and ignition occurred. It was a mighty blast indeed, the other three tanks were blown off their supports, pipes and valves ruptured, gas poured freely into the air, multiple explosions followed, it was a veritable inferno with geysers of flame. The Priest was sitting meditating on the loo, having just completed a rather relaxing shit, when the blasts occurred. High pressure waves were generated and the multiple stresses were more than the small building could bear. The roof was blasted to pieces, masonry disintegrated, and a piece of concrete slid towards the head of the Priest, he saw it coming and said, Holy Mother of God, then impact occurred, and he died.

C'est Finis.

So marching onwards to white-out, it ends what has barely begun, it begins what will shortly end, the stream of time cheating me of time, yet it is now in my place to be the Judge. The Air Vice Marshal I shall send to Hell immediately on account of the countless boys he has ravished, and in any case he was recently an atheist, which is actually trivial, for when he sees me he will believe soon enough, I would have been lenient on account of he being a real sport deep down despite the Boer in him and all that, but the sodomising of young boys, why I must maintain the track record, to Hell with him, oh well I must consider all the effort that the Priest put in, performing the last rites and all that, anointing him with Holy Oil prayed over by no less than the Popeye himself, alright, to purgatory then, purgatory for the Air Vice

Marshal, and may his misery be small. Now the Priest, his is a delicate matter. I will call him into this room and look at him standing speechless before me. Finding his voice he will say in a shocked whisper, You were God all the time? Gently, I: Indeed, I know you were sorely tried. His record is very good, the Priest, excellent compared with other mortals, his only failing being breasts, which he adores, he has a collection of photos tucked away in a cabinet, and it is a rather splendid effort, thousands of glossy photos, and why would I begrudge such a simple failing, in the end he only sighs and remembers Fuseina, a Muslim girl he had fallen for in the days of his youth, indeed she was well endowed where breasts were concerned, doubtless this was the reason for his fixation, his proclivity was for the breasts of young black women, he was racist in that regard, should I hold that against him? well no! Seeing how he suffered to remain pure and virgin even when faced with the pudendum of Fuseina, which test he passed admirably, he did not fornicate, ho no not this young man, and witness him crying in the morning mist outside the departure lounge in the airport as the aircraft, a Boeing from British Caledonian it was, roared off into the sky with Fuseina in it, Fuseina to some cold, cold part of Canada forever, and the cold crept into his heart and gnawed, and from that moment onwards all that was possible was the Holy Orders and at the end of his life a collection of photos of breasts and one can feel sorry for the Priest because Fuseina's breasts were missing from the collection, had he had hers the collection would not have grown, well a mortal would have thought that but God cannot be deceived, the Priest is sitting in the room at the other side, he is getting restless but does he not know that we have eternity, I can judge him for a thousand years and still not have finished, but let me now call him, the Priest, and let us be done with it all.

THE PENITENT

EVERYBODY MUST BE angry with me.

No, disappointed. However, it is God that I am worried about, what He thinks about me, and what He intends to do with me, and what remediation is possible.

There are things. The bleeding Heart of Christ. The Crown of Thorns. These images. Rosary. Count the beads to penance. Count, the beads: *Pray for us sinners now and at the hour of our death*, when all memories come crowding in.

I am drowning. Is this water? Is this blood? Why can't I float? Perhaps no buoyancy. Heavy with sin, with doubt, Peter reaching for the Christ, the Christ sure on his feet on the water, who could match his powers? no one.

This water. This baptism.

In a college apartment in New Orleans there was this girl, a student, of liberal arts, or economics, or women's studies, memory fades. And upstairs the other students were having an orgy and the wooden beams creaked. She giggled and said something random. Shaqueen she was called. No, she was not black, or there was another, Julia she was called, white, with brown hair, auburn, her lipstick did not smudge. She must have laughed, too, and said, But this is ridiculous. The fixture trembled and shadows shifted.

I cried. No, not then, but later, later, when the wood was dry, beholding in my mind from a distant hill God hanging from the tree at the time that the wood was green.

This water. This blood. This wine.

Later, later, when it was getting close to the end, an all-night walk, wandering disturbed through the meandering streets and by-ways and paths in Darkuman, there was a dog that suddenly appeared, seeking a companion. Strutting along the gutter edge. Some boys were sharing a joint in front of a lotto kiosk. They watched him with beady, perhaps sympathetic, eyes, this lost soul wondering *how did I get to this point.*

It was a mistake. A wrong turn on the fork. But it was written in the stars, predestined, was it not. But was there truly no return from this path, when the decision only involved a telephone call. And I couldn't remember the number. And heartbreak followed. And hatred. Was that the turning point or just one of several turning points, each one more wrong than the preceding. Six useless numbers, and couldn't remember. I'm sorry! Forgive me. I did not mean to. Circumstances. Telephone. She was waiting for the call. And the days turned to weeks and the weeks to months. Mercy.

Censer. Incense. Crucifix.

Jesus, Jesus. They were praying in the spirit that night in the park in Darkuman, would not let the neighbourhood sleep, why should sinners sleep, it is better to pray than to sleep, Hell-fire don't you know, must escape at all cost, why, God's opinion is the one that really matters, all else is vanity, this water, this blood.

Rosary. Five decades, of life, of errors, looking back, what a waste, shit, how could I have, God, but I am guilty and not forgiven, in New Orleans she was naked, a minor in economics, and the wind beat against the panes.

The pornography industry is a CIA operation, Omar said. Just like weed in colleges. I am for Allah! You fekking Kufr, why bring me to this perfidious point. I have since come to see the kind of escape he sought as he leapt from the window, Omar. The hostel room was on the tenth floor, the streets of Jersey were quiet that Sunday, what have I done he cried what have I done as he disappeared leaving the besotted party gaping, and the sheriff shouted he had had enough of them fucking niggers and it never ends, eh. O for a miracle, Omar: Allahu Akbar! cried the crowd of fascinated onlookers as angels bore him upward. Yet it was only the broken body on the side-walk and it was not even an escape.

The engine rumbled as the air-conditioner compressor came on. The lips. The zip. The strands of one hundred per cent human hair were getting in the way. Did I make you happy? I think so. At the time. I couldn't care less, now. It was not enduring, hence, worthless. All is vanity.

In New Orleans the power of gris-gris heaved in the air. Crack cocaine is just something that niggers do. The rest do blow. The heater rattled as the blower came on. Smoke hung in the small room. Shaqueen or Julia tossed another Bud. The beams creaked on account of the exertions upstairs.

This is how it ends, there is no mercy. No bargains with death. One day I'll be laying in state, if lucky, if not booted out of an aircraft by angry stewardesses peeved at such blatant sexism, that black pervert in the aisle seat, the ape in 27E, totally uncivilised, straight from the jungle, he had the gall to do this, and do that, away with him, drag him to the door screaming, shark food, and all this while flying over the

Atlantic, the pilots obliging with low altitude and low speed on account of de-pressurisation, outraged co-passengers in mob support, tar and feathers, the Osama treatment.

Her name was Shaqueen, no Julia, she was Latino, a voter beloved of the Democrats, her husband was away in Afghanistan, she was coveted, flowers did the trick perhaps, and thou shalt not commit adultery, regardless of the width of the hips, the tremblous boobs, and the bouncy brown hair with that oh summer! smell. Every rose has its thorn, wormwood, nuclear radiation poison and the rabbit with six legs. Thou shalt, and Thou shalt not, ten times, spot on, why Lord, you know man too well, too well. Yet how easy to break all ten. All ten.

This life. This water. This blood.

The terrible yellow of those walls. The aged, wasted flesh, the joint sucked dry. The smell of stale smoke. The narrow bed. The little loo. The little window high up there. The machine that controls our lives.

Step forward. Who do you think you are talking to? It doesn't matter. It's all over.

The life that cannot be lived anymore. She said the church was a cult of guilt. A bastion of oppression. The oppression of women. Smoke curled from her lips. Why do the priests wear skirts? Her name was Shaqueen.

This water. At the end of the stick the sponge levitated, to mouth, this wine, this centurion, this cross. For the sins of the world. Christ did you know what you were letting yourself in for? Do you forgive also the silent drone strikes and the kinetic actions and the shock and awesomeness and the women trapped in cellars for years by incestuous demand and the abortion holocaust and the men that lie with men? and do you forgive me, a sinner, ripping my garment apart at the temple, and do you forgive me, a sinner, spouting disbelief over vodka?

The telephone. The disconnect.

In Alavanyo there is a small church, left by the Germans thanks be to God, the musty smell of the confessional, the priestly robes rustle as they brush against the wooden panels of the cage. The priest shaking his head in the gloom. This confession I can no longer hear. This confession no priest can hear. This sin cannot be absolved. Prepare for eternal damnation. What can we do but pray, pray! This priest turning away, the hollow sound of the door closing on the confessional, yet you cannot say you didn't have your chance.

This blood. This water.

On the radio he sounded convincing, but it was only his voice, because what he said I could scarce believe. What does it mean that Christ died for us? The thing to understand is that the magnitude of the sacrifice was not the cross, painful as it might have been, neither the humiliation, bad enough as that was, nor even the fact of his innocence, for many others have died in that manner, the preacher said, crossing his legs. I had gone to see him in his office. It is the fact that he who is God was accused of and punished for all the sin of the world past present and future, this is the terrible fact of the sacrifice represented by the cross. You are a sinner but you are free to go. I will not be punished? I am forgiven? I need not pay? Not even if you could, this preacher said, he was a fat man with thick lips and a receding hairline. Yet how could I be free? the body is the temple of the Lord and in New Jersey they passed weed and blow around and in New Orleans the liberated economics major showed her powers by stripping to her thong, and the floor boards upstairs creaked on account of the bacchanalia paid for by the CIA, all hail the sorority, but it could not be right on account of the bombs falling at the other side of the world at that very minute, and children blasted to glory to secure this great freedom which was spent in dissipation.

So this preacher with his worn-out Bible and get out of hell free card you're saved anyway, what did that mean I mused, not then but later, and what about hell and heaven and judgement and were those not important they are in the Bible too, for where then would the tears be wept and the teeth be gnashed? Where then the outer darkness and from whence then the smoke of the burning that rises for ever and ever? and the smoke of whose burning? And was the grace sufficient whether or not I admitted my sin, for it is appointed unto man once to die, for all have sinned and come short of the glory, and let he who is without sin cast the first stone, and Jesus scrawling in the dirt with a stick, and who could match the Christ for class, where are your accusers the Lord asked, and neither do I condemn you he said, and he had not even died yet, much less risen.

Lord have mercy. In the tract received on the bus today the warning is stark. When He comes again He will not be so kind. You gonna face the music, you really gonna pay for all the shit you've done, better get out now while there is still time. Don't let this chance pass you by.

It was dry, dusty, brisk, the sun was blinding. The cross was heavy and the rough wooden beam bit into his shoulder, and blood spilled from the bruises and seeped into the seamless garment, and it itched where the thorns bit the flesh, and a cruel thorn plunged into the flesh above the right eyebrow, and his knees hurt and his back stung from the stripes and stung worse where flies settled in to suck blood, and he knew, that this was the world that he had made, and these were the descendants of Adam and Eve, and the end of the cross struck a rock and he staggered, and lost his balance, and Jesus Falls The Second Time. Hail Mary, full of grace. Holy Mary, mother of God.

If you stop looking at me I shall go away and not say another word.

There was a brass band. A boy on the lead trumpet. Dust to dust. This world. This coffin. This life. This end. This blood. This water. Of life. Thou shalt not kill, that knife, that pill, the blood. No other gods. That prayer. That appeal. The demons. Satan in the shadows, the deceiver ever ready to receive.

Yet how easy to break all ten. All ten. This life.

I cannot help it. I'm hooked. I'm lost. You cannot save me.

The things I'll never forget. This life. This blood. This water.

Procession up the dirt road in a box, this corpse, riding in Sunday best, deathday best, burial best, the flesh dissolves and the bones are clad in mouldy cloth, give it some time and you will see, the end of this body, of sin.

Can't you see my sins are eating me up? Mercy. Can't you see that I have repented? Can't you see I put my hand to the wheel? Can't you see I looked back? This pillar of salt, and brimstone like hailstones, flaming from on high.

Good morning. The hum you hear is the air-conditioner, and also, the fluorescent lights. You will soon get used to the sound, and then you will no longer hear it. You will soon get used to the pain, and then you will not feel it. You will soon get used to getting used to it, and then you will no longer be used to it. Where are you from? Where were you born? The introduction. This life. This water. This blood.

It cannot be so. How can I pay? Do I want to pay? Or do I mean pay now and escape eternal hell, and when I meet those that I wronged on Earth in Heaven will I still say sorry?

Take a deep breath and try again. Do you know how it feels. Time heals all wounds. Time destroys all healing. This is the memory machine. It hums, throbs, runs. Follow the arrow, go up the steps, turn to the right. In the corner a man sat smoking. Let he who has no sin cast the first stone. Go and sin no more. All ye that are weary. My yoke is easy. My burden light.

I shall walk on my knees from Odawna to Nsawam. Have mercy on me, a sinner! My knees on the rough asphalt, and I will be bruised and I will bleed and the Sun will burn and I will thirst, will this be enough will I be free from the past the haunting echoes of my deeds and when I get to Nsawam after several days on my knees on the road the skin would have stripped and the flesh would be bloody, would this be enough? I will throw myself into the Densu, will this be enough penance Lord, if I suffer and die for my own sin? But how to suffer and die for the original sin, too, that must touch the impossible, yet the baptism at birth, that took care of that, so the baptism at death...

Lord have mercy.

How would I like the coolness of the chalice on my lips.

How I would like the coolness.

The chalice.

My lips.

This wine.

This blood.

THE CWROLING CATERPILLAR

A NAKED MAN was standing on top of a hill formed by a massive outcrop of granite which reared all its four hundred and fifty feet abruptly from a large body of water.

The dull sky diffused a grainy light over the entire landscape, and in the dreary illumination distant objects were smudged out, smeared into the greyness of it all.

A terrible expanse of black, barren rock, smooth and unbroken in some places, shattered and craggy in others, the product of cataclysmic events involving violent explosions and magma, rolled away from the hill as far as the horizon in three cardinal directions. In the fourth direction was the water, so vast that it was an ocean, yet so still and untroubled on the surface that it could only be a lake. The rock on which the man stood sloped downwards with an uneven grade and plunged into the lake, and seen from the shore, the man was a mere speck. A fine and athletic specimen of the species, he was five feet and seven inches tall, his broad chest undulating with firm muscles that also defined the topography of his flat stomach, his compact biceps and sturdy legs that terminated in bare feet with slightly splayed toes. He stood still, calmly scanning the surface of the lake, his eyes moving from left to right, and from right to left, as he painstakingly examined the distant horizon beyond the waters. And he had been doing this for a long time.

A boat made its way along the lake, moving steadily in a straight line, propelled by the steady strokes of a paddle wielded by a figure seated at the stern. When the man on the rock spotted the boat it appeared as a mere dot in the great distance, an almost indeterminate little blob on the horizon, emerging like a sort of mirage in greyscale. But having seen the boat the man began a descent to the shore. He moved carefully, choosing each step with caution because the rock surface was rough and undulating and a foot set down poorly could cause a perilous precipitation downwards.

The boat reached the shore while the naked man was still making his way down the rock face. The pilot, placing a steadying hand on the gunwale, disembarked. He was carrying a staff. For a short while he stood at full length, imperious, like a commander reviewing the guard, the staff in his right hand rising one foot above his six foot height. The staff, straight and brazen in appearance, was topped off with a pearly ovoid, making it look like a blunt spear.

His cloak, made from some fine, metallic yarn, had a large stiff collar that reached up to his ears. The collar was in the shape of an inverted cone, opening in a V at the throat so that his round, shaven head looked like a cannon ball nestling in a rigid funnel. Forty-four buttons closed the cloak from the neck to the hem.

The man made his way to the foot of the outcrop, striking the ground with the staff at each step. He stopped and raised his head, the better to see the naked man in his laborious, cautious descent to the shore. He waited unmoving, like a statue cast in steel.

In due course the naked man reached the bottom of the incline and proceeded along the shore until he reached the man with the staff, and the two men stood face to face. The naked man was a head shorter than his opposite, who now inclined his bony head downwards and said 'Greetings!' and his voice boomed across the shore and carried over the hill, which replied with a slight, flat echo, greetings... greetings... greetings...

The naked man did not say anything in reply. The man with the staff spoke again, quietly, dropping his chin slightly so that his line of sight grazed the bald dome of the naked man's head. 'You have travelled far, I know this. I have been kept informed of your progress, since I am one of your keepers for this trip. As a matter of fact, I am the last keeper that you will meet, and it is my duty to take you to your final destination. By now you must be aware that, according to the protocol, I must make it clear to you how irredeemable your situation is, and emphasise that it is impossible for you to retrace your steps. In any case all that exists for you apart from the terrible nothing, are featureless monoliths of some sort, like the rock behind you or the lake before you, extending for distances better measured in astronomical units. It is also my duty to remind you that you will never again meet another human being, or animal, living or dead.' He paused, then half-turning, pointed at the boat with the staff. 'Now we shall sail. Come!' The last word was again spoken in a loud voice, booming across the shore as before and reflecting weakly off the rock, come... come... come...

The two men climbed into the boat and sat face-to-face, the naked man at the bow facing the stern, and the keeper at the stern facing the bow. Laying the staff carefully at the bottom of the boat, the keeper picked up the paddle and sent the boat sliding into deeper waters with a powerful shove. Then he thrust the paddle into the calm water, barely rippling the surface and making no sound at all. He dipped first to the left, then to the right – and his tireless arms propelled them at a steady pace, and in time the shore was lost in the all-encompassing grey. They moved in silence, travelling in a straight line as before. There was no wind blowing, and even though they went a great distance, the sky remained the same dour grey colour, diffusing the same grainy grey light.

A rounded hill appeared above the surface of the water. It was an island, cutting a precise arc in perspective, a darker grey shadow over the grey surface of the lake. This was initially only visible to the keeper, seated aft. However, the island grew larger and larger as they got closer, and when they reached the shore it was clear that the island was of great extent indeed. The surface of the island was a dull concrete grey, and it followed the curvature of a circle where it met the water – it was in the shape of a hemisphere. The boat struck the edge of the island with a hard thud, and rocking slightly, came to rest. The two men climbed ashore.

'Here we are,' said the keeper. He placed his right foot against the edge of the boat and pushed. He did not seem to put much effort into it, but with a slight scraping sound the vessel slid back into the water and made off steadily, moving at such a pace that it was clear it would travel a great distance before it would, perhaps, become motionless somewhere on the lake. They watched for a while as the boat disappeared from view, and then they turned and made their way up the smooth surface of the island. The grade was gentle and rose steadily, unlike the outcrop on the other shore.

Presently they reached a hole in the ground. It presented a black circular profile about three feet in diameter. 'We go down,' the keeper said, pointing with the staff at the hole. 'Jump. Your feet will meet a surface, it is not too deep.' Seeing that the naked man did not move, he added, 'You falter, you hesitate? Perhaps it might make you feel better if you could picture, in your mind, the geography of our current location? If so, I shall describe what we have here. Imagine, if you will, a building that is a sphere, the outer diameter of which is the diameter of a small planet. You cannot imagine? Very well, you soon shall see things for yourself. Here we are at the outer wall of this building, and as you can see, it is almost fully submerged in the lake. We are here, as it were, at the main entrance to the building.' The man pointed again at the black circle in front of them.

'This building is made of concentric spheres, which form the floors, as you might want to put it. The floors are made of solid granite and are several feet thick. On every floor, there is a hole such as this that leads to the floor below. Through these holes we will descend by jumping, there being neither stairs nor elevators at hand. Now – and this is not to scare you – but just as a matter of fact, there are six hundred and sixty-six floors in the building. And we shall keep going down towards the centre of the sphere, until we have passed all these floors. Then, at last, you will be at your destination.' The naked man hesitated. Without saying another word the keeper stepped backward and applied the end of the staff to the left cheek of the traveller's arse. 'Afraid!' the keeper shouted, and increased the pressure on the buttock. 'Afraid? Now? With what you have already seen? Afraid? Now? With what is still to come? This is not the time to fear.' And then with a swift motion, he pushed the naked man into the hole, and the blackness welled up all around him. He fell through the air, arms flailing, and landed on his feet, staggered with arms outstretched for support, found none, and fell flat on his face. There was a soft rustle and a thump as the keeper landed beside him. A short silence followed, and suddenly the two men were bathed in a pool of soft white light, streaming from the ovoid at the top of the staff. But the light was not very bright, and only illuminated a few yards into the gloom ahead.

'This is the first level,' the keeper said, making a sweeping motion with his staff. 'We will keep descending, and at level six hundred and sixty-six, far down below, we will reach the room that has been prepared for you. But now we have to find the entrance to the next level. We need to walk.' He led the way, holding the staff with the lamp pointing forward. His boots hit the floor with a metallic clack-clack. And the two figures trod on in the stillness, illuminated by the pool of light, their shadows thrown down against the floor behind them. There were no walls in any direction.

And so they came to another circular hole in the ground. Like the first hole, it was about three feet in diameter, but the blackness of this hole seemed more intense than the blackness of the first. Again they jumped into the hole, the naked man first, then the keeper, and again they walked until they reached the third hole in the ground.

This sequence of events was repeated six hundred and sixty-three times, the brutal monotony broken by nothing, neither speech nor change in circumstance, except that each hole appeared darker than the one before, and when they stood at the final hole the blackness seemed to spill out of it, smudging the circumference and heaving gently, like a pillow of smoke. 'So we stand at last at the entrance to your room, your final destination. It is a dungeon, make no mistake, but you will find that it is better appointed than you might expect. It is a large room, of course – space was never in short supply – and you can walk great distances in any direction. But be not deceived, for even though there are no walls escape is impossible, because the floor of your room is the surface of a sphere, and all paths will eventually bring you back where you started. Please jump.' But the naked man did not jump until he was prodded with the staff, and when he entered the hole he fell for a long time before crashing onto a hard surface. After a while the man with the staff jumped down as well, the light at the end of the staff gleaming like a star, rapidly brightening until he landed on his feet with a loud thump.

'Stand up,' he said to the naked man, who lay sprawled on the floor. 'Let me show you around.'

The keeper showed the naked man a desk placed a little way to their right. It was a fine desk, made of some dark red wood. The polished top gleamed dully under the pool of light cast by the ovoid on the staff. 'You must not think that all effort has been directed towards some sort of punishment for you,' the keeper began. 'Indeed, if you consider the situation carefully, you might find that this is not the case. For example, you see here on the desk a notebook and a pencil. You can write all you want, and when the pencil is spent, a new one will be ready in the top drawer. Likewise, when the notebook is full, a new one will be ready in the second drawer. If you want more illumination at the desk, touch up the reading light.' The man prodded the desk with his staff, and then pointed at the reading lamp, sleek on its fine silvery neck. It started to glow, casting a shaft of light onto the desk 'You see, the light is a warm, cheerful amber. And look, by this little wheel you can alter the hue, the sharpness, and the brightness. I must mention that it is an item of the highest technology. It is powered by a battery that lasts forever, and holds a lamp that burns forever.

'But do take note that there is no chair behind the desk. Indeed, there is no chair inside the room. I trust this will not discourage you from putting your thoughts down on paper, an exercise that sustained countless incarcerated men during the centuries of the execrable civilizations that human beings inflicted on the universe. However, even though you can write all that you want, you cannot turn the pages backwards to read what you have written, no, the pages only turn forward. I am sure that this is only a small inconvenience, since, being the author, everything you write should be in your memory and you will miss nothing if you are unable to turn the pages backward. Just like time is supposed by some to flow: Forward, Ever! Backwards, never! Speaking of which, I present the clock.' At the right hand side of the desk there was a desk clock, the sweeping curves of the carved wood encasing a pearly white circular face behind transparent sapphire, with Roman numerals marking the hours, and hands glowing a sharp cobalt blue. 'Another item of high technology,' the keeper continued. 'It only loses one second a millennia, a loss which though small is of significance in terms of eternity. But as you will recall, a simple time piece counts to twelve hours, and then starts again, and this is all it does. The reason why you have a simple clock is as follows. To count the days will engender desperation in no time at all, as you will agree. To count the seconds, the minutes, the hours, yes, that is meaningful, a circular representation of the linear progression of time, yes, that should be bearable.'

Then with a sweep of his staff, the keeper illuminated a section of the floor. He motioned the naked man to come closer, and when they stood shoulder to shoulder, he pointed to a tiny dark spot on the ground. The light from the ovoid became more intense. 'Look,' he said. Clinging to the rough stone was what looked like a spider, but it had a tail with a sting at the end, like some type of minuscule scorpion. It had also had wings. 'And finally,' the man said, 'I introduce you to the Crwoling caterpillar. Why is it called a caterpillar? Perhaps it was a caterpillar at some point during its creation. Despite its name it is not a living thing, it is of the nature of a virus. However, it is like an insect in many respects. It is small, it flies, and it bites. It has a most painful bite, which it bites at random. It does not bite to feed or to defend itself, it bites only to inflict pain. This it does perhaps once or twice in a day – perfectly at random, of course. It can be crushed if you are swift enough. However, destroying it leads only to a brief reprieve, because it subsequently resurrects and in doing so, replicates, such that there will then be two Crwoling caterpillars instead of one, both with exactly the same characteristics, save that one of them will thereafter be indestructible. A little game might serve to entertain you, and in some way help ease the passage of time, if that is meaningful. It is a thinking game of great relevance, as you shall see. Here it is. If you destroy fifteen Crwoling caterpillars, how many indestructible ones would you have spawned? And how many Crwoling caterpillars would there be then? If one Crwoling caterpillar is happy to bite one bite every twenty-four hours, how many bites in a day will you suffer after destroying fifteen of these creatures?'

The keeper turned to face his naked companion. He straightened up, his legs together, the hem of his cloak casting a sharp shadow over the tips of his boots.

'But now my work is done,' he said. 'Yet, lest you entertain the foolish notion that escape is in some way possible – whither I cannot tell, but then again eternity is a long time indeed, and even the most worthless ideas might seem cogent – I shall myself make no attempt to return the way we came. It is just not possible to do so. For even if I were by some ingenious device able to propel myself upwards to the next level of this building, I would need to find the path to the hole leading to the level above that. But I could not do that, for the simple reason that each of the six hundred and sixty-six spheres have recently spun, and randomly so, and the positions of the entrances have altered greatly. However, granted that I was able to pass through each of the six hundred and sixty-five other holes, and thereby reach the surface of the island, how would I then cross the lake without the boat? And if I were by some miracle able to cross the lake, and climb the rock, how would I get lifted off the plateau to the other terminal, there being no more transports provided? And how, most importantly, would I arrange it, that even as time progresses, everything else at least stays fixed, so that I should meet all as it was before? Indeed, it is an impossible undertaking to return.

'And now having delivered you to this place, the purpose of my existence has been achieved, and I am no longer useful. Therefore,' – the keeper raised his staff and struck the floor violently with its foot, leaving the shivering staff embedded in the floor like a lamp-post, its ovoid head still shedding light – 'here it ends, for me, but not for you, for whom there is no end.' The keeper took a few steps backwards, his hands clasped over his midriff. He stopped when he was about two yards behind the staff. The light fell fully on the cloak and the smooth metal fabric threw back the light in cold, baleful rays. His eyes, underneath the bony overhang the sockets, glimmered in the direction of the naked man who stood silent before him. 'Do you have anything to say?' the keeper asked. 'About anything? Do you have a question? About the past, perhaps? You wonder how all this was made? You want to know if it was also made in six days? And why it was made? And by whom, really? And whether it could be otherwise? And where all the other people are?

'No? Nothing?' The keeper paused and held the silence for a while. Then he said again, softly, almost to himself, 'No. Nothing.' He turned slightly away from the naked man and touched the neck of his cloak, hesitating briefly before unfastening the first button, but thereafter in steady succession the remaining forty-three buttons were undone, and the keeper removed his cloak and cast it aside. The garment disintegrated as it fell. There was nothing underneath the cloak, and when the keeper kicked off his boots which vanished in the parabolic rise, the naked man saw that there were no feet either.

Then the keeper's neck crumbled into dust, followed by his head, fine dust falling in a thin line to the floor, where it made a small grey heap.

And that was all.